HIS
BABY

TRESSIE LOCKWOOD

AMIRA PRESS

BABY

Amira Press
Charlotte, NC
www.amirapress.com

Chapter One

Tae tucked her bare feet beneath her on the couch and answered her cell phone on the third ring, more than enough not to sound too eager. "Hello?"

"Hey, beautiful, what's up?"

She rolled her eyes but couldn't stop the grin spreading over her face. "Nothing much, stranger. What have you been up to?"

"The usual."

She laughed and brought one foot out to study the polish on her toes. A pedicure was long overdue, but she tended to put them off in favor of getting more work done. Not like she dated anyone right now to care one way or another. "You mean eating executives for breakfast, right?" she teased her friend, Daniel—*ex*-boyfriend.

"Who me? Never." The deep rumble to his voice washed over her like a caress, one she remembered all too well.

"Please, who are you kidding, Daniel? This is me. You forget I know you better than anyone. You didn't make VP at your company by the time you were thirty playing tiddledywinks."

"Do you know me so well?"

He paused, and she could have sworn he flirted, hoping she'd fall into his trap and admit she still had feelings for him. Tae licked her lips and pulled in a quiet breath. No matter how tempting, she would not give in. The ship they had been on together had sailed three years ago. They were good friends now and nothing more. Besides, the last she'd heard he dated some slinky blonde with big boobs and a body to kill for. Tae glanced down at her own figure, a healthy size fourteen, and figured the competition was too fierce to even get in the game.

"What if I said you're no longer the one who knows me best?"

A twinge in her heart made her frown. He couldn't know the impact of his words. "What do you mean by that?"

"I'm—wow, I never imagined saying it to you of all people would be so rough, and weird."

Alarm bells went off in her head. "Dude, you're scaring me. Just blurt it out."

"Octavia." He always said her full name when he was being serious. Her throat dried. "I'm getting married."

"Oh wow! Are you kidding?" She infused her tone with bubbly happiness. "That's so awesome. I'm glad for you. Is it the same woman you were dating when I ran into you at Cosmos?"

"Thanks." He chuckled. "No, that was a phase. This is Alise. She's great, Tae, and I can't believe she said yes. I want you to meet her and get to know her. You'll love her. That's why I'm calling. Say you'll come to the wedding. I need one of my best friend's there to celebrate with me."

He sounded happy, so she put aside her petty issues. Daniel hadn't broken it off with her. She'd dumped him, and he had remained her friend. He never treated her badly after the breakup. That said a lot about the kind of man he was, and he deserved as many good things in his life as possible. In fact, she was a fool for letting him escape.

"Of course I'll be there. Nothing can keep me away. Jax your best man?"

"None other."

"Oh goodness, you're going to let that man near all the single women at your wedding? They'll get ideas in their heads, and Jax will encourage them—right into his bed."

Daniel laughed.

"Unless you're telling me he's changed?" She stood up from the living room couch and headed toward the kitchen.

"No, he's still a womanizer."

"A player," Tae corrected, shaking her head. "Well, just be warned because you don't want the drama on your special day."

"At least it will be memorable," he teased.

"I'll give you that."

She spoke to him a little while longer, updating him on work, and he filled her in on a few details of his fiancée. Tae found herself looking forward to seeing this woman who had captured Daniel, but when the emotions bubbled too close to the surface, she made an excuse to get him off the phone and disconnected.

The next call she made was to her best friend, Zerita.

"Hey, girl," Zerita chirped, always bubbly.

"Hey," Tae echoed.

"Uh-oh, who pissed in your Cheerios?"

Tae rolled her eyes and opened a cabinet door over the kitchen counter. "Must you be crass, nut? I'm just calling to tell you the news."

"What news?"

Tae pulled down a box of cereal and opened it. Grabbing a bowl from the dish rack, which she hadn't emptied after washing the dishes, she searched a drawer for a large spoon. "Daniel's getting married."

Zerita gasped. "You mean your Danny?"

"He's not my Danny, but yes, my ex."

"The one you've been pretending to be friends with but in reality you still love him, Danny?"

3

"For real, Zerita?" She filled her bowl with cereal and then considered getting a bigger one out of the cabinet. "I am not still in love with him." She lied. If there was one thing about Tae, she did not lie to herself. She did love Daniel, but she had no intention of admitting the fact to Zerita.

"Are you eating Frosted Flakes?"

Tae froze with the box clutched in her hand. "For your information, I'm in the living room realizing I need a mani-pedi."

"Listen, woman," her friend intoned, "unlike normal people who eat ice cream or doughnuts when they're upset, Frosted Flakes is your comfort food, and I hear you crunching in my ear. So don't try to play me talking about you don't love Danny."

Tae moved the phone away from her mouth so she could munch the cereal in her mouth without Zerita hearing. When she'd swallowed, she brought the phone back to her face and then searched the refrigerator for something to wash down the dry cereal. A cola appealed, so she grabbed one and popped it open.

"I'm the one who broke it off after he asked me to marry him, Zerita, or don't you remember that?"

"I remember." The *click* of the keyboard sounded in Tae's ear, and she knew even though it was Sunday, Zerita wrote her column for the magazine where they both worked. "You weren't ready to get married."

Tae nodded despite the fact that her friend couldn't see her. "Thank you. I'm glad you've got your facts straight. I am not pining over Daniel Elliott."

"Uhm." Zerita sounded unconvinced. "So he called to tell you. Did he want you to beg him not to do it?"

"Would you stop? No, he invited me."

"And you told him no, right?"

"I told him I'd be there with bells on."

Silence.

"Zerita, are you still there?"

"Seriously, Tae, I'm not sure about this. I wasn't sure about the two of you staying friends and hanging out. I mean there are unresolved feelings there. I know you like to pretend you don't still love him…"

"He's in love, Zerita. He's getting married."

"Everybody doesn't get married for the right reasons."

"You act like I'm the only woman he'll ever love. I'm not that vain, and you know I don't believe in that soul-mate stuff."

Her friend sighed. Tae heard the tapping pause. "I'm not saying I think he's the one for you. I don't know if he is, or he isn't. Last time we all hung out uptown, I saw the way he looked at you, and that wasn't so long ago. If he really is in love, it was either his longing to have a family that brought it about, or he's just tired of waiting for you."

"Speak your mind, why don't you."

"Girlfriend, you know I don't mince words. It's what makes me a damn good writer."

"Toot toot!"

Zerita laughed. "Whatever. Anyway, please do me a favor and think about this. When is it?"

"A month from now."

"Wow, they're not wasting any time. A small event?"

Tae glanced down at her thighs, encased in leggings. She hated how big they appeared, gathering most of the extra fat on her body, and she pushed the bowl of cereal away. "I had the impression he waited until almost the last minute to invite me. His fiancée has her family coming in from Baltimore, where she's from. Everybody is staying at the Hilton out on J.M. Keyes."

"That's a decent hotel."

"Yeah, I figured I'd get a room out there for the weekend too because Daniel said they were going to have a party the night before and of course the reception following. I don't want to drive across the city half-drunk late at night."

"That makes sense."

"Well look let me let you go, Zerita. I have to take care of a couple things, and then I'm going to go to the gym for an hour or two."

"Uh-huh. Gotta get in shape for that wedding."

Tae made a rude noise. "I've been meaning to go, and I have the membership going to waste."

"Whatever you say." The tapping started up again, rapid fire. "Talk to you later. Keep me updated on if you change your mind."

"I won't—change my mind that is. Talk to you tomorrow. Maybe we can do lunch on Monday."

"Sounds like a plan."

"Bye, girl."

❖

One month later…

Tae carried her garment bag over her arm, along with a small suitcase as she strode to the check-in counter at the Hilton. The diminutive woman behind the counter aimed a bright smile at Tae. "Welcome to the Hilton. How are you today, ma'am?"

"Good, thanks," Tae responded. "I'm Octavia Croft, and I have a reservation."

"Of course, Ms. Croft. One moment, please."

Tae set her suitcase down and rotated her shoulder. Tension locked the muscles across her upper back, and she debated taking the muscle relaxer Zerita had given her before she set out to come to the hotel. Then again, she preferred to enjoy the effects once she'd unwound in her room and kicked off her shoes with a drink in her hand.

"Tae."

The deep, scratchy, but without question sexy, voice came from behind her, and she identified its owner before she spun to face him. Rather, she turned to face his chest. Jaxon Hart stood several inches taller, towering above her with a barrel chest, massive arms, and a handsome face. His voice paired with his devastating, dark good looks had women dropping their panties left and right, and he had encouraged it from the first day she met him.

"Hey, Jax," she said, a little breathless as she always was around him. "You're here early. I thought everyone was coming in on Thursday." Tae had elected to take a rare day off to arrive at the hotel on Wednesday. She'd thought to lounge around the hotel alone for her mini-vacation before she had to be social with people she didn't know.

Jax smiled, flashing the most perfect white teeth she'd ever seen. Then again, they could compare to Daniel's. The best friends were perfect foils for each other—Jax dark, Daniel light.

"Didn't Daniel tell you the wedding party would be arriving on Wednesday for a last-minute rehearsal?"

She bit off a groan. "No, I should have realized that. The last wedding I attended was my sister's ten years ago."

"You're looking beautiful as usual," he commented, sweeping his gaze from her head to her feet. Tae found herself toying with her hair, which she'd crimped and dyed bronze. She'd thought the color a bit too stark, but it fit with her caramel skin tone, so she didn't fret too much. Maybe she didn't look as hippy as usual either. After all, her crazy exercise regimen over the last thirty days had whittled her waist down by a couple inches and lost her ten pounds.

She blushed at his compliment. "Thanks. You're not looking so bad yourself."

"From you that always sounds like an insult."

"I don't know what you mean, sir." No way would she tell him flat out how hot he was. The man's head might explode. She squinted at him. "Is your head bigger than usual?"

"You cut me, Tae." He rested a hand dramatically to his chest. "I'm not what you think I am."

"So you brought a girlfriend with you?"

She thought she'd cornered him, but he stepped closer and took her hand. A chill raced over her skin, bringing goose bumps up on her arms. "I'm all alone. Would you fill in?"

"Not on your life, pal." She tugged her hand free of his grasp and turned back to the counter. Once her business was done, she refused help with her bags and started toward the bank of elevators. Jax, strolling with the casual grace of a jungle cat, joined her. She peered over at him from the corner of her eye and took in the short-sleeved shirt that hugged powerful arms at the biceps and his slacks, which hugged narrow hips but gave room to the generous rise at the crotch.

"Are you checking me out, Tae?"

She jumped at hearing his low, sexy voice and frowned at him. "Of course not."

"Hm." He winked at her and held the elevator door open while she passed by him. His fingertips grazed her lower back for just a second until she moved away on the pretext of pressing the button for her floor.

"How is the private-investigations business going?" she asked. "Any interesting cases?"

"Every now and then. Often it's following cheating spouses and gathering evidence for divorce court."

She shook her head. "Great, more reason not to get married."

He gazed at her. "That why you turned our guy down three years ago?"

She sighed. "Jeez, does everyone know my history?"

"Everyone like who?"

"Never mind."

He moved closer, and all of a sudden the elevator seemed no bigger than a small closet. The scent of his aftershave tickled her nose, or it could have been cologne. Either way, he smelled yummy. She took a deep breath, finding no reason not to enjoy it for the moment. The problem originated with his charm and how he used it at every opportunity, on every woman, including her. She knew he didn't mean anything by it, that it was just his way, but Jax was a temptation for any hot-blooded woman who hadn't had sex with anything other than her vibrator for too damn long.

"Are you still in love with him?"

The question caught her off guard and ripped her from her thoughts. Odd that at that moment she'd been thinking of touching Jax and not of Daniel. The question couldn't have been more ill timed. "Why would you ask me that?"

"It's a question."

"I know, but—"

"I've known you both for a long time," he said, "and I watched the two of you together. You loved him, and he practically survived off every word that fell from those beautiful lips."

She put her hand on her hip. "Are you trying to guilt-trip me?"

"Not at all." When he touched a hand to her cheek, she gasped and stared up at him. "If you still love him, this will be hard for you, seeing him marry someone else."

The unexpected empathy blew her away. Never in a million years would she have thought Jax would say such a thing to her. He and she were friends, but they never did more than flirt and tease. They didn't hang out except when he'd double date with whatever woman had caught his fancy at the time with her and Daniel. He had always seemed nice but shallow.

She lowered her gaze and pulled out of his grasp. "I'm fine. Thanks. What Daniel and I had is in the past. I appreciate your concern."

The elevator dinged a floor before hers. Jax reached out to play with a lock of her hair. A tingle of awareness raced through her system. "I like how you keep changing it, black one week, red the next, blond after that."

She suppressed a grin. "You don't see me often enough to know if that's true."

"Have dinner with me tonight."

The elevator doors slid open just as she opened her mouth to turn him down. Words died on her lips when she came face-to-face with Daniel, an older woman, and a younger woman who could be her sister.

Chapter Two

"Tae, you're here."

"Hey, Daniel." Tae didn't get to finish her greeting before he dragged her off the elevator and into a bear hug. If she'd been aware of Jax's sexy presence a moment ago, Daniel's overwhelmed her senses and weakened her knees. His big arms encircling her generated both a feeling of comfort and one of panic. She pasted a smile on her face and fought to get free of his hold, stepping back when she did to put space between them. Despite the distance, her nostrils were filled with her ex-boyfriend's scent, and all it did was evoke memory after memory of their time together.

"Let me introduce you to Alise," he was saying, but Tae focused on the man himself. As usual, Daniel wore a suit. She'd teased him many times that he lived in them. Only when they dated had she convinced him to dress down. They'd had to shop for sandals for him the one time she had unbent enough to take him to a family reunion.

Daniel's blond hair had been cut recently, she assumed, by the way it lay in perfect order. She'd always preferred it a little longer and somewhat disheveled, what she'd called the fresh-from-bed look. Only a hot white guy could pull off the look, and

Daniel could, but that wasn't his style. His blue eyes shone with happiness, and she had a twinge of jealousy, which she stomped down to pay attention to his words.

"This is my fiancée, Alise Harper and her mother Mrs. Juanita Harper. Alise and Juanita, this is a good friend of mine, Octavia Croft, but everyone calls her Tae."

Alise wrinkled a cute little nose with a dusting of freckles on it. "What kind of name is Octavia?" Her skin tone was a close match to Tae's if a hair lighter, and Tae suspected the wave in her hair didn't come from a flat iron. Tall with long shapely legs, shown off in a minidress, the woman made Tae the cheap knockoff to the original, but her snooty attitude left a lot to be desired.

"It's the kind of name my father gave me," Tae snapped. "It was my grandmother's name."

"Alise," Daniel scolded.

"Oh, sorry," she said with clear insincerity. "I get pissy when I'm hungry. Danny, you know I don't like waiting."

Tae looked from Alise to Daniel to Jax, whose expression held amusement. Was Daniel seriously going to marry this chick? Tae drew in a breath and blew it out. She decided to extend Alise the benefit of the doubt. Maybe this was just prewedding jitters. Yeah, that must be it.

"Well, it's nice to meet you both," Tae said between clenched teeth. "If you all will excuse me, I'm going to get settled in my room."

Daniel grabbed Tae's hand, saw the evil glare Alise gave him, and dropped it like a hot potato. "Tae, if you don't have any plans for dinner, why don't you join us?"

"I—"

Jax's big hands settled on her arms. She'd forgotten he stood behind her and about his offer. "She's agreed to have dinner with me."

Tae gave him a break and didn't call him out on the lie, but Daniel's smile seemed forced. She noted the annoyance in his gaze. "The more the merrier. I made reservations at Nakato."

"I thought you didn't need reservations there," Tae said.

Daniel smiled and took Alise's hand in his. "I wanted to be sure everything worked out perfectly and there wasn't a wait.

Of course, or she'd pitch a fit.

"Oh okay. Um, I don't want to horn in on your time…"

"I'm not taking no for an answer, Tae, so put your stuff in your room. We'll be in the lobby."

She suppressed a sigh.

"I'll help you," Jax told her.

"I don't need—"

He shuffled her down the hall, and the impatient Alise dragged Daniel toward the elevator. Tae recognized a losing battle and gave in. Twenty minutes later, she, Daniel, Jax, and Alise and her mother sat around a table with a hibachi grill in the middle of it, waiting for their personal chef to begin his show while preparing their food.

The chef began his routine tapping his fork and metal spatula on the grill in a smooth rhythm to capture all of their attention. He swung the utensils around, flipped them in the air, and ducked his head beneath them a few times. Tae and Jax clapped and cheered. Daniel smiled, and Alise appeared less than impressed while she clung to Daniel's arm as if someone might steal him away. Tae wasn't sure if Mrs. Harper was awake.

Piles of veggies were added to the grill, atop a generous amount of oil, then shrimp. Tae always enjoyed watching how the chef's hands blurred as he prepared the shrimp. He sent the meat to one pile and flicked the tails in another direction. When he was done, he flipped the tails so they disappeared. She had no idea where they landed. Next, he carefully compiled a volcano made of onion. He poured vodka and olive oil into the center. Tae glanced at Alise, but the woman paid the chef no mind. The little volcano went up on fire, and Tae whooped.

"You're like a little kid, easily entertained," Jax whispered in her ear.

She punched his arm. "You liked it, too. Don't lie."

He shrugged. "I never pretended to be mature."

"Idiot." She laughed at him, and he grinned back. Tae noted how Alise placed a manicured nail beneath Daniel's chin and directed his attention toward her. She said something too low to hear, and Daniel's blue gaze flashed with interest. Tae looked down at her hands, barren of any rings. She'd taken them off that morning to wash a few dishes and forgot to put them back on. Three years ago when she told Daniel she couldn't marry him, she had asked herself a million times if she made the right choice. Every so often, she reaffirmed, if only to herself, that the decision had been right for her.

"You're missing the show," Jax said.

She looked up, but the chef could no longer keep her focus. Determined to keep a positive outlook, she turned to Jax. His green eyes, which always held a sense of mystery, were trained on her. Right now, the knowing they reflected pissed her off, but she swallowed the emotion. "Is work ever dangerous?"

He hesitated, and at first she thought he'd call her on the attempt to distract herself and him, but he gave in. "Sometimes. Not long ago, I followed a guy whose wife believed he was having an affair."

"Was he?"

"No, that's the thing." Jax frowned, remembering. "He had an addiction to gambling—*illegal* gambling—and I stumbled onto the people he owed money. A case of mistaken identity."

The wince as if he recalled pain made her put her hand on his arm. "Oh wow, you didn't get hurt too badly, did you? I guess you didn't considering you look okay to me."

Jax leaned in closer. "You like the way I look, Tae?"

"Does your mind ever leave the gutter?"

"Where's the fun in that?"

She smirked and shook her head. "So what did they do?"

He shrugged. "Cracked a rib, a few bruises. Nothing I couldn't handle."

"Of course."

They chatted some more, and then Daniel drew them into conversation, entertaining and charming all rolled into one. When she got her food, Tae shifted it around her plate, half listening to the conversation around her. Only when she couldn't avoid it did she join in. Old emotions, insecurity, questions, all bubbled up inside her regarding Daniel, and what made it worse was he seemed so oblivious of how confused he made her. One minute he looked at Alise as if she were his world, and that was the way it should be. The next he said something Tae and no one else would know the meaning of, directing a devastating smile at her that she had to fight a reaction to with all her might.

After one such instance, Jax bumped her arm with his. "You okay?"

She made a small sound of dismissal and waved her fork. "Please, I'm having a great time." Internally, she groaned. *Why would I say that? It sounds stupid.*

For once, Jax didn't tease her, and she was grateful to him.

Halfway through the meal, several ladies called out to Alise from across the restaurant, and for the first time that evening, Alise perked up, a smile spreading over her face as she waved the three women—two white and one black—over to their table. "At last my friends are here," Alise gushed. "This boring dinner will have some life."

Tae's mouth fell open, and her eyes widened. "She did not just—"

Jax grabbed Tae's hand and drew it into his lap. "Let it go," he murmured under his breath.

Tae frowned at him. "You've got to be kidding," she whispered back while the others were talking. "She didn't just diss us. She disrespected Daniel. If he's that boring, why is she marrying him?"

"Tae." His stern tone was enough to snap her out of her anger, and she shut her mouth so fast her teeth clicked, sending a sharp pain through her jaw.

She opened her purse and pulled out her wallet. "I think I've had enough for one evening. I'm going to go back to my room. You all enjoy yourselves. Daniel, this should be enough for my part of the check."

Daniel leaned across the table and closed her fingers over the money she tried to hand him. A tingle of awareness raced from her fingertips, across her hand, and up her arm. "Don't insult me offering to pay, and don't leave. I was thinking we'd all go across to the hotel bar and have a few drinks."

"I'm really tired," she lied. "Thanks though. I'll see you in the morning."

Tae tugged her hand free of his and stood up. Jax started to rise, but she held him where he was. "Good night. Thank you for dinner, Daniel."

Before anyone could say more, or for that matter before *she* could, she hightailed it out of the restaurant. With luck, the rest of the weekend would go better. She would wish Daniel all the happiness in the world and walk away.

❋

Tae checked the minifridge in her room and then realized she'd need to go to the ice machine. On the way, she could grab a cola and some chips from the snack machine. *Tomorrow, no next week, I'm going to get healthy and start exercising.*

She rifled through her purse and found change, but it probably wasn't enough, so she pealed off a few dollar bills from the thin stack in her wallet.

Standing in front of the vending machine, balancing the ice bucket on her hip, she debated between Cheetos, her favorite, and Doritos, her second best.

"Still a snack junkie, I see."

Tae jumped, and Daniel squeezed her shoulder. Her heartbeat skidded out of control. "Daniel, I didn't hear you behind me."

"Sorry about that." He smiled, taking her breath away. "I didn't mean to scare you."

"No worries." She forced her gaze back to the chips, but with him beside her, she didn't want to buy anything. "Alise not with you? I thought you two were joined at the hip." The bucket clattered to the floor and she slapped a hand over her lip, bending to retrieve it. "Damn, I didn't mean—"

"You don't like her." His words were a statement, but she heard his disappointment.

"What I think doesn't matter. Besides, I shouldn't have said anything. This is your weekend, and I'm not going to get in the way of that."

He took the crumpled dollars from her clammy fingers, smoothed them, and fed them into the machine. While she said nothing, he made the selection for her, choosing the Cheetos. "You're my friend, Tae. I care about what you think."

She took the offered snack and her change, biting her lip. Warning bells went off in her head. *Keep your mouth shut, Tae. Wish him well. That's it. Then get your butt back to your room where it's safe.* "Are you sure about her, Daniel? Marriage is a big commitment, and she doesn't seem… Well, she seems selfish. Does she love you? Do you love her?"

"Love," he repeated.

She had said too much. Why couldn't she mind her own business?

He frowned, his eyes flashing anger. "You talk to me about love, Tae? You turned me down when I asked you to marry me. No, you didn't just say no or tell me you weren't ready. You dumped me completely, without warning. Now what are you after? Why are you here? To stop me from being happy? Maybe you want to get back together after all this time."

She retreated a step. "Excuse me? You invited me!"

He reached for her. "Tae—"

She held up a hand. "I'm sorry. I made a mistake." She spun on her heel and hurried away, leaving her ice bucket. Let him keep it. Why oh why had she thought this was a good idea? Then to be accused of trying to break Daniel and Alise up because she wanted him back. That was absurd, and she hated knowing he thought that way. His anger was uncalled for, too. He suspected how she felt. Hell, he'd have to be blind and an idiot to think anyone in their right might would like that self-centered bitch he intended to marry.

Tae swiped her key card five times and jiggled the doorknob at her room. Each instance, the stupid light flashed red. She heard steps around the corner, and her heart raced, dread tightening the muscles in her stomach. She didn't want to face him again and have him see the tears in her eyes. *Stupid, stupid, stupid!*

She tried the card again and this time threw the Cheetos on the floor along with the cola. Now the stupid drink would explode when she opened it. She sniffed and swiped a hand across her face. The door swung inward, and she pitched forward and banged her mouth on a hard chest. Squeaking in pain, she tried to right herself, when hands came up to her waist to steady her.

"You want to tell me why you're crying and trying to break into my room, Tae?"

She glanced up in to Jax's face, then at the number on the door and realized too late she'd stopped at the wrong door. "Um, my bad."

She spun to walk away, but he moved in front of her and stooped to gather her snacks. When he had them in hand, he placed fingers at her lower back to guide her farther into his room. The door shut, the automatic lock clicking into place.

Chapter Three

"Here." Jax pressed a glass into her hand, filled with ice and an amber liquid. "Drink it."

Tae sniffed the beverage and wrinkled her nose. "I only drink vodka."

In answer he placed a finger on the bottom of the glass and tilted it toward her lips. Tae took a small sip, and the alcohol burned its way down her throat. Even though the taste was horrible, the effect was immediate. She felt light-headed but a little more relaxed. Another sip warmed her belly, and she walked over to take a seat at the table. Jax's room matched hers, but where she'd folded her things into the dresser, from the looks of it, he'd left his in his suitcase. At least he'd hung a garment bag in the open closet, which she assumed carried his clothes for the wedding. The jacket and shirt he'd worn earlier that evening had been slung over a chair, and he stood bare-chested and barefoot.

"Aren't you going to put some clothes on?" she questioned him, casting her gaze away from him.

"You're the one who invaded my room."

"I believe *you* abducted *me*."

He grinned, and she matched it with one of her own. "That's better. No more tears but tell me. Why were you crying?"

"I wasn't," she lied, and then she sighed. Another sip of the drink, and he nabbed it from her hands. She frowned. "I wasn't done with that."

"I see it going to your head."

She waved a hand. "I'm fine." The slightest slur to her words made her wonder if he was right. "If you must know, I was falsely accused of trying to break up Daniel and Alise."

Jax's brows rose toward his hairline. "By who, Alise?"

She giggled. "That would have been drama, wouldn't it? No, by Daniel."

"Tae." Jax's voice held a warning.

She clenched her hands into fists. "Don't 'Tae' me. I did not try to break them up! I would never do anything to hurt Daniel."

"But you admit you still love him."

She fell silent and looked away.

Jax strode over to the minifridge and rummaged inside. In a few minutes he'd made her another drink, this time just orange juice. Tae accepted it with her thanks. Jax made something for himself, downed it in a couple swallows, and poured another. He took the seat opposite her, and Tae put her glass up to her mouth. Over the edge, she took in his wide chest, noting the smooth and taut skin with no hair. She liked a hairless chest rather than the carpets some men sported.

"I'm your friend too," Jax said. "Talk to me."

"We've never had a confession type of relationship."

"No reason we can't start now."

She kicked her sandals off and drew her feet up. Jax looked down at her toes, and she was thankful she'd gotten a pedicure before coming. "I do have unresolved feelings for him. That's not a crime." Damn, she sounded defensive, but Jax waited for her to continue. "He asked what I thought of her. I told him I didn't see the love."

"Fuck, tell me you didn't say that, Tae."

She couldn't help the whimper. "I did. I'm such an idiot. I promise you, it wasn't my intention to break them up. When I turned down Daniel's proposal, I thought I was doing the right thing."

A curious expression came on his countenance, one she couldn't identify. He set his glass down and toyed with it. "So you feel you made a mistake?"

"I didn't say that."

"You're not denying it."

"He's getting married, Jax. Whatever I feel doesn't matter. Anyway, I don't know why I'm telling you all this. You're his best friend."

His green gaze met hers. "What you tell me tonight is between me and you."

"Really?"

"Scout's honor."

"Boy, please. You were never a scout."

He chuckled and winked. Her nerves settled a bit more.

"Since you shared with me, I'll do the same."

Tae tilted her head to the side, studying him. Jax had always seemed open about what he wanted. He didn't bite his tongue or go along with the crowd. He had no shame even when others tried to judge him. One would wait an eternity for an apology for being what he was. "You have secrets? Don't tell me you don't like Alise either. No, wait. You do like her, and you've been keeping it from Daniel, heartbroken that you'll never get to be with her."

"Funny."

She shrugged. "Anything's possible."

"Sure," he agreed. "You're right. The woman I'm interested in does belong to Daniel, in a sense."

"I don't get it. Is there some oth—" She froze. "Are you serious?"

"Is it so hard to believe? You're incredibly beautiful and very sexy. Does my admission disgust you?" When he looked at her breasts, she resisted raising a hand to them, both turned on by his interest and confused by it. She and Jax had always flirted, but she'd never thought he was for real. Just because Daniel had dated black women didn't mean Jax would find them attractive enough to take to bed.

She cast her gaze toward the floor, a tingle starting between her legs that she'd like to blame on the alcohol. "Not at all."

Jax stood up to make her another drink, this time with vodka, and Tae accepted it. She took her feet out from under her and crossed one leg over the other. Jax downed another drink and stretched his arms over his head. The bastard knew what he did, she thought, amused as she watched the ripple of corded muscle.

"Have you been with anyone since Daniel?"

She choked on her drink and pounded her chest coughing. Jax rushed over and patted her back. He brushed close to her side, and she felt the heat from his body, but only concern registered in his expression. "Are you okay?"

"I'm fine. Thanks."

"You can ignore my question."

"No, I haven't," she admitted after a few minutes of silence.

Jax hadn't moved from the side of her chair. Now he leaned over her, his mouth so close she felt his hot breath on her neck. She dared not look up at him, but he had no such qualms when he grasped her chin and raised it. A tremor raced through her body at his touch, but still she kept her lashes lowered. Jax's thumb teased her bottom lip, and she had the most ridiculous desire to suck on it.

"You need to get him out of your system."

She didn't know what made her say, "I suppose you think you're the one to do it?"

He closed the breath of space between them and kissed her. Tae's lips parted of their own accord, and she dipped her head farther back before her mind caught up with what she did. She raised her hands to push him away, but her will snagged on the feel of his warm skin beneath her fingertips.

"Make no mistake," he intoned, "if I took you, another man would not enter your mind."

"Y-You…" She cleared her throat. "You're pretty confident. Every man can't please me sexually." What the heck was she saying? No way she'd show a man of Jax's physical perfection her lumpy body with the stretch marks and cottage-cheese thighs. Hell, she'd been terrified of showing Daniel, but when she did, she'd been a size smaller, and he loved her at the time.

Jax dropped a hand to her shoulder and then moved it down her arm until he reached her hip. When he slid it around to her belly, her pussy clenched. She bit her lip as he massaged a spot above her clit, not even touching it, but so close it drove her insane.

"I could drop to my knees right now and eat you until you scream."

She shivered and shut her eyes. "I should go back to my room."

"Is that what you want?"

"Um."

He pinched the button open on her jeans and lowered the zipper. She had a sudden urge to say if they were going to have sex, she needed the light turned off. That would deny her too. She wanted to see him, to take in his sexy body and to see his cock. From the beginning, even when she and Daniel were hot and heavy, she'd noticed how Jax had seemed to be hung. Were women dropping at his feet because he had everything they wanted and knew how to use it? Or did he have the equipment and thought he knew how to please a woman but was more about getting his? She couldn't help desiring to find out for herself.

Jax eased a hand inside her jeans, and she didn't stop him. He flattened his palm against her pussy on the outside of her panties. His fingers pressed to her bud and her slit, but he didn't go farther than that. He nibbled her earlobe, tugged it between his teeth, and then licked the sensitive spot behind it. She arched against him, her eyes shut.

"You don't have to be nervous," he whispered.

Her eyes flew open. "I'm not."

He drew away and looked into her face. She stared back, and the denial died on her lips. "Is this the charm you use to get what you want?"

He smiled. "I've been with all types of women."

Wow, she didn't care to hear that, but it sobered her. If she wanted this, the decision would be a conscious one, with an awareness that this was about sexual pleasure, forgetting the past, and like Jax said, getting Daniel out of her system.

Well, here goes nothing.

Tae pushed Jax back, and he didn't resist. He pulled his hand out of her pants and stood. Tae did as well, and she crossed her arms to grab both sides of her T-shirt to pull over her head.

Jax's moan a low rumble, he stretched a finger toward her bra and hooked the tip between her breasts. A slight tug told her of his eagerness to get a better view. "Take it off."

She swallowed. Her breasts weren't as perky as they'd been before she hit thirty a year ago, but they weren't bad either. She liked the D cups. They were heavy, and her nipples were nice and big. After dropping the bra to the floor, she waited for his reaction.

"Damn," he muttered. She could tell nothing from the one word until he cupped her breasts, weighing them in large palms, his gaze locked onto her nipples. Just having him stare like that sent an arrow of desire between her legs and made the small buds pucker in readiness of his touch. Jax still held her breasts in his hands when he brushed thumbs over the tips. He said no more but stepped closer and lowered his head. She anticipated the pleasure, her lashes fluttering and her head dipping back. He closed lips over one nipple, and she cried out. Her reaction must have unhinged his need because he snaked an arm around her waist and jerked her off her feet, crushing her against his length. With her feet dangling in the air, he devoured her breast, at first kissing the swollen mound and then sucking the peak between hungry lips. He flicked his tongue across the most sensitive area and then captured it to bite down. Tae dug her fingernails into his shoulders, gasping for breath. She couldn't believe she came so close to an orgasm, and she wasn't even naked yet.

"I've been wanting you a long time," Jax growled when he raised his head. The intensity in his gaze made her shiver. "Now I'm going to have you, and I'm not stopping until my need has been sated."

He set her on her feet, and she put her hands on her hips, tilting her head to the side. "What about my need?"

Jax unbuttoned his slacks and lowered the zipper. She licked her lips when he reached into the gap and produced a thick and long cock that made her mouth water and hands ache to wrap around it. He raised a dark brow in question. "Do you actually think I cannot satisfy you with this?"

Tae panted. Even his confidence turned her on. He reached for her hand and closed her fingers around his the smooth erection. The shaft pulsed under her touch, and Jax forced her to slide her palm up and down its length. He placed pressure over her fingers when she reached the head and made her give it a squeeze. When she did, he dropped his head forward and moaned.

He kept one of her hands trapped beneath his and raised the other to her cheek, grazing her bottom lip with his thumb. "You're going to please me, and I'm going to make you scream my name. Is it a deal?"

Hell, yes!

"Hm, I don't know. I'm not much of a screamer."

"Then I will show you what you've been missing. Take off your jeans."

Now was the crucial moment. Tae almost chewed off the flesh on the inside of her cheek as she bent to push her jeans over her hips and slide them down her legs. Even while her pussy wept with come, eager to feel him buried inside, she worried about her thighs. She dropped the pants on the floor and stepped out of them, her attention focused somewhere between his throat and his chest.

"Lose the panties, Tae."

She swallowed. There was nothing of the romantic in Jax, but she didn't care about that. She didn't need or want him to pretend he loved her. He stood in front of her watching every movement. She slid the panties over wide hips and down her thighs. Her pussy came into view, trimmed short but not bald.

"Turn a little."

She did, and he stared at her ass as she stepped out of the panties and tossed them on a chair. By this time, between her legs had practically transformed into a fountain. Of course her thoughts exaggerated the situation, but the man made her hot. What could she do?

Jax ran a hand over her ass, gave one cheek a squeeze, and then raised his hand. He stopped midmovement. "Are you okay with me spanking you?"

Tae shuddered. "If you get off on it."

"You don't?"

"I'm not sure." No man had spanked her before.

"I'm an ass man, and yours is perfect. Along with those luscious thighs, I'm about to burst before I get in you." He turned her to face the table and placed her hands on the top. Crowding her from behind, he nuzzled her neck and nipped the skin gently between his teeth. "Sometimes I get a little rough."

She tried not to collapse on the floor. Jax dipped his knees and brought his cock to her butt. He grasped her hip and drove her back to him as he pushed forward. She moaned. He crossed an arm over her chest from behind and cupped her breast, pinching the nipple between two fingers.

"I won't hurt you unless you want me to—but just a little. Is that acceptable?"

The verdict in, she'd never had a lover like Jax, and joking around with him all these years hadn't given her a clue to his real nature. Excitement churned in her belly, and she peered at him over her shoulder.

"I'm all for it. Let's go."

Chapter Four

Jax held Tae at her waist and tossed her onto the bed. She marveled at his strength, but the thought didn't last beyond his dropping to his knees and thrusting her thighs apart. She drew in a shaky breath as he examined her apex. A finger traced from her navel, down to her mound, and then to her clit. His feather touch sent chills racing over her flesh, but a whimper ripped from her throat when he thumbed her nether lips open and licked her dripping come.

She gasped. "J-Jax."

"First I'm going to make you come," he said, "because I love the taste of come, and your pussy is soaked. Not to mention your smell."

She frowned. "My smell?"

He breathed deep, his nose almost buried between her slit. "Mm, pungent and good."

He pushed one of her legs higher so her ass rose off the bed. A greedy swipe of his tongue along her pussy had her shaking. She even felt the bubbling of a scream but suppressed it, deciding it was his suggestion and the way he talked to her that brought on the temptation. Jax leaned up, his eyes trained on her pussy. When he smacked her butt, she jerked in surprise.

His gaze flicked from between her legs to her face. She stared back at him, and he spanked her again. She drew in a sharp breath. He did it again, and this time, her core muscles contracted as if in direct response. Jax cast her a knowing glance before he dove between her legs and began eating her out with gusto.

His moans, the way his tongue flicked over her slit and how he sucked her bud between his lips all worked together to send her into orbit. She squirmed, but he held her down, not allowing her to move as he took what he wanted. The noises he made with his mouth, the slickness of her pussy, brought her to the brink of an orgasm. She tangled her fingers into the sheets and pumped against his face. He licked her clit faster and then stuck his tongue inside her, wiggling it around. The ability to breathe fled. She grasped her knees and held them as high as they would go, opening her pussy wide to him. Jax took the invite and laved until she couldn't stand it anymore. She writhed on the bed, whimpering his name. Her orgasm crested and erupted. Tremors rocked her from her core and extended to consume her body and mind.

Jax planted several kisses on her pussy and then sat up. His narrowed eyes and pinched mouth said he wasn't happy.

"What's wrong?" Her stomach muscles clenched.

He waggled a finger at her. "You didn't scream. That means I have to try harder."

"I'm sorry, but I said—"

He whipped her to her feet and marched her toward a bare spot at the wall. "Grab the wall."

"But—"

The *crack* of his hand over her ass cheek sounded in the room. She jumped. The hit stung, but Jax rubbed it out. The moment the burn faded away, he smacked her ass again. This time she did as he asked, so turned on she could barely control her movements. Jax stood behind her and tangled fingers in her hair. He gave a light tug that made her dip her head back and reached with his other hand beneath her ass. His fingers found her front entrance, and Tae went up to her toes. He parted her lips and wet his digits then skimmed them along her slit. Tae panted. Jax teased her, alternating between dipping inside of her and playing with her pussy lips. He stimulated every nerve ending and then let go of her hair so he could bend down and reach farther between her legs. He jerked upward until she rested her weight on his forearm.

"J-Jax," she moaned.

Slowly, he drew back, sliding her pussy over his arm. Where he'd eaten all her come a few moments ago, now she was wet all over again.

"What are you doing?"

"Ride it," he demanded.

"I can't."

"Grind on my arm. Do it now, or I'm going to spank you harder than I did before."

A tingle of both fear and excitement ignited in her being. She began moving on his arm, arching as much as she could manage in her awkward position. Pushing her ass out, she braced herself on the wall and then pumped. The movement grazed her swollen pussy lips and had her keening with pleasure. She ground on him a little harder.

The sensation drove rational thought from her head. All she could focus on was riding his thick arm, teasing her body. Inner muscles clenched and unclenched. Jax murmured encouragement, his words raw and sexual. He moved close and spoke less than an inch from her ear, the heat from his breath raising goose bumps on her arms.

"Feels good, doesn't it?" he whispered.

"Mm," she agreed.

"No matter how hard you ride it, you can't seem to come, can you?"

"Don't tease me."

"Do you want my cock inside you, Tae?"

"Yes!"

"How badly do you want it?"

"Very bad!"

He fisted his hand and slid his arm backward between her legs. She bit down on a shout when his fist bumped her clit, but she held onto it, rubbing her body against him. A *clink* of his belt sounded in her ears, followed by the rustle of clothing. To her whine of protest, he removed his arm, but she didn't have to suffer long. Jax nudged her feet until she spread them farther apart. He held her around the waist, and the tip of his cock nudged her entrance.

"Tae," he murmured.

She glanced over her shoulder, and at the same time he took her mouth, he plunged his cock into her pussy. His thrust, so painful, almost violent, robbed her of strength. She lost her grip on the wall, but he slung an arm over her chest and drove her back to him, holding her up while pushing his shaft deep inside her. She'd misjudged his size because he stretched her walls and filled her to capacity. His invasion gave no apology but demanded her surrender. Together they leaned on the wall, the chill bringing bumps to Tae's arms and legs. He squeezed her in his embrace and thrust his hips to drive his dick farther. Tae shuddered, not even able to speak his name this time.

His lips touched the shell of her ear. "Do you want me to stop?" He drew his shaft almost all the way out and plunged back in. She sagged in his hold.

"No, don't."

His fingers found her clit, and he pinched until it stung. Air hissed between her teeth.

"You're going to scream for me."

"I don't think…" The words died on her lips. He placed her hands back on the wall and pushed from behind until her breasts touched the chilly surface. An arm settled around her waist as if to protect her hip bones, and then he began a slow grind into her. The rhythm picked up speed, going faster and faster yet controlled. Sensations Tae had never experienced jangled her nerve endings. Every time Jax drove into her, he seemed to bump a spot that both took her strength and rocketed her closer to climax. She clenched her jaw and breathed through her nose. Still, his onslaught continued. He grunted dirty words designed to ignite her lust. Oh how they worked, she thought, whimpering.

Jax pinched her clit, tugged it, and pushed fingers into her wetness atop his own cock. She howled in pleasure, but it wasn't quite a scream. They were in a hotel, and there was no way she'd let herself get too loud no matter how good he made her feel.

Tae neared release, and she put her head on Jax's shoulder, ready to let go. "I'm going to come again. It feels so good, Jax."

His voice was a rumble above her head. "Mm, I like you saying my name. How about a little louder for me, baby, and I will give you everything?"

She licked his chin and explored higher to his mouth. His bottom lip found its way between hers, and she sucked it. "No way."

"No?"

He slowed his thrusts, and she frowned. "I'm close. You're not going to deny me, are you?"

For an answer, he pushed two fingers deeper into her pussy beside his cock. She grabbed his forearm, the hard muscle shifting beneath her hold. His strength reminded her of how he lifted her, and the size of his arm brought back memories of humping it. Her pussy throbbed, contracting so tight, any second her orgasm would explode.

Jax still moved slower, and she complained. "Please, fast like before."

"Do I have your permission to ravage your sweet body in any way I see fit, as long as I don't hurt you too much?"

Drunk from his loving, she nodded. "Don't stop. Please, don't stop."

The next instant, he pulled out of her pussy and whipped her around to face him. He thumped her against the wall and followed, plunging his cock between her legs. His gaze locked with hers, and she couldn't look away.

"Tae, baby, I'm about to come!"

He raised one of her legs and drove his shaft hard and deep into her heat. The other hand he splayed on her ass separated her cheeks. She had just enough time to realize what he intended before his digit sliced into her anus. The scream as she climaxed must have been heard stories below in the hotel lobby. The next instant, his hot come filled her.

Tae woke and scanned the darkened room. Where was she? Then she remembered, the hotel, Daniel getting married. Wait, this wasn't her room. A sheet barely covered her naked body, and a heavy, hairy leg covered one of hers. She pushed it away and looked to her left. The hand she slapped over her mouth suppressed the cry of alarm, thank goodness.

Jax lay on his back, no sheet whatsoever giving him modesty. He stretched out naked as the day he was born, and even as his chest rose and fell, and he snored just a tiny bit, the man still looked confident.

She rolled over and landed on her feet at the bedside. Regret washed over her. What had she been thinking having sex with him? Everybody knew about the unspoken rule of not sleeping with the best friend of exes. Maybe if she left now, no one else would find out about it. No harm, no foul. She peered at the clock on the nightstand and almost groaned that it was just after three in the morning. Everyone should be in bed. She searched the dark room and found her panties, jeans, and T-shirt but not her bra.

Damn, where the hell is it?

When searching took too long, she decided to write it off. Besides, if Jax found it, he would not be so stupid as to return it in front of everyone—she hoped. With her shoes in her hand, she tiptoed to the door, checked the hall, and then hurried out. Her room lay two doors down, meaning either she was seriously upset when she tried breaking into Jax's or she'd subconsciously been jonesing for him all along. *The first reason!* she decided. Sex with Jax had been good though, insanely good. Her sore body testified to the fact. She could and would spend many nights after this one remembering the experience, but under no circumstances would she ever repeat it. Maybe in the morning she'd also ask Jax not to tell anyone it happened. He would respect her wishes.

At her bedroom door, she slipped her card into the slot, and this time it worked without issue. She opened the door and tossed her sandals on the floor.

"Tae, what are you doing?"

She froze and turned slowly. Daniel stood in his doorway across the hall, dressed in pajama bottoms and a T-shirt. His feet were bare, and his hair was tussled as if he'd been asleep. Had she made too much noise?

"I…uh…" she stuttered.

He folded his arms over his chest and grinned. "The snack machine again?"

She frowned and straightened her back. "I'm not healthy, but I don't wake up in the middle of the night to eat!" Too late she realized she should have jumped on the excuse. Better that than the real reason she had just returned to her room.

Daniel offered a gentle, understanding smile and raised his hands in surrender. "I'm not judging you. I was wondering if I could talk to you."

He crossed the hall toward her, and her eyes widened. A whiff of his shower gel reached her long before he did, and her knees weakened a bit. She backed away. "It's late, Daniel."

He caught the door as it began closing. She'd made the mistake of moving into her own room, and he followed. "I want to apologize."

"This isn't a good idea."

"A minute. I promise."

The door clicked shut with Daniel on the inside. Tae stood still, hugging herself. She hadn't showered before returning to her room. Thoughts of Jax's scent all over her body arrested her movements and kept her from thinking straight. "Daniel…"

"I was wrong, Tae. I shouldn't have accused you of being jealous. All you've ever been after we broke up was my friend, and I don't want to ruin that. I don't want to go into my marriage with this over my head."

Tae relented. "Don't worry about it. It's not that serious. Besides, maybe I was a little jealous. After all, Alise is a lucky woman, right?"

He drew her into a hug, and she stiffened in his arms. A wash of memories rolled over her, and for a second she let them, laying her head on his shoulder.

"We're good?" he asked.

"Yeah." Her voice came out raspy. "We're good."

She walked with him to the door and held it while he passed through. He made a few more comments, but she looked down the hall. Had she seen movement, or was it her overwrought imagination? All of the wedding party occupied this floor, including Alise, Alise's mother, and the bridesmaids and groomsmen. That fact alone made it crazy that she'd even thought of sleeping with Jax. Well, it was over, disaster averted. She would put the pleasant memory with Jax in the past, along with all she had shared with Daniel, and wish Daniel well for his future. She said good night to him and then turned into her room to grab a few more hours of sleep before the activities of the weekend celebration began.

Chapter Five

"Miss Octavia Croft! Is Miss Octavia Croft present?" the high-pitched voice called. Tae winced and weaved her way around a small crowd of people milling about. She'd wanted to stay out of sight until the reception dinner, but apparently that wouldn't be possible.

"I'm Tae Croft," she said to the slender man in the gray suit holding what looked like a very expensive camera. "You bellowed?"

"Tae."

She turned and found Daniel approaching. Her breath hitched in her throat, and he grabbed her hand. "Come on. I want you in the photos."

Her eyes widened, and she tried tugging her hand away. "Are you nuts? I'm not in the wedding party."

Alise moved up beside Daniel and stared daggers at Tae. Tae blinked at her. *You need to check your husband, not me.* Tae was the one who had been accosted.

"Alise and I want to take pictures with our best friends," Daniel assured her. "You and Jax are mine, so it's our turn. Come on."

Tae held back, but a hand started her feet in the direction Daniel wanted her. Jax appeared at her side, a smile gracing his handsome face. "By all means, bro. This is your day."

Alise's displeasure shifted to Jax, and he hurried to correct himself, amusement plain in his eyes. "I mean you know aside from Alise, of course."

"Of course," Tae muttered and ignored the response she got from the bride.

Moments later, she somehow ended up behind Daniel, her hands on his waist, and Jax behind her, his hands on her waist, all of them turned to the side, face toward the camera. Both men were ridiculously tall, so she felt like the meat to their bread, which wouldn't be a bad thing in a fantasy, but not just after Daniel's wedding. She willed the photographer and his assistant to hurry with the photos.

"Okay, now just you three." The photographer pointed to Daniel, her, and Jax.

"Daniel," Alise protested.

"Sweetheart, you took pictures with your friends."

"Mine weren't...*her*."

Tae sighed. "You know what, I'm out." She tried to walk away, but Jax caught her hand and dragged her back.

"It's a picture, Tae," Jax said under his breath.

"Why do you sound like I'm the one with the problem?" she bit back.

Alise and her girlfriends glared so hard Tae thought she'd catch fire at any second. She could only imagine how the pictures would come out, her in the middle of Daniel and Jax, miserable and trapped. The second all the clicking ended, Tae muttered an excuse and exited the room. She jetted down the hall and found the ladies' room. Shoving the door wide, she paused at the small crowd and backed out. Another door farther down merited investigation, and she ducked her head in. A conference room presented itself. She slipped in and shut the door behind her, sighing. Her due diligence as Daniel's friend had been done. She could leave and skip the reception. After everyone headed into the room where she'd spotted the congratulatory sign for the happy couple, and then she would make her escape.

While she leaned against the wall with her eyes closed and biding her time, the door next to her clicked open. Tae groaned and turned to see who disturbed her peace. Alise stood in the archway, offense radiating until the baby's breath weaved into her silky locks quivered. She stepped into the room and shut the door behind her.

"You and I need to talk," she quipped.

Tae yawned, touching the back of her fingers to her mouth. "I disagree. Nothing you have to say interests me. Go find your husband."

Alise bristled. "What did you say to me?"

"Did I stutter?"

Alise stepped closer, but Tae raised a finger.

"Back up."

"What?"

"Three seconds."

The woman seemed to rethink getting in Tae's face and returned to the door. "I'm not going there with you. I see the kind of woman you are, and I'm not letting you ruin my wedding day."

"You don't know me to say a word about the kind of woman I am, but I wouldn't ruin anybody's wedding day. I think it should be perfect in every way, something to look back on. As Daniel's friend, I support him."

"His friend?" Alise put her hands on her hips and laughed. "Who do you think you're fooling? I know you want him back, but it's too late. See this ring? It says Danny's mine. You lost."

Tae shook her head. "I didn't know this was a contest, but since you know your husband so well, why don't you know he hates being called Danny?"

Alise paled, and Tae pressed her advantage.

"Yeah, that's right, but you don't care, do you?"

"I love him! And he loves me calling him Danny. It's our thing." The simpering turned Tae's stomach. She should have left no matter who didn't like it. "I know you're jealous. He told me how he broke up with you, and you kept chasing after him trying to get back together."

Tae clenched her jaw. "Oh is that right?"

"Yeah, that's right." Alise touched a long French-tipped nail to her red lips. "I'm glad you came. Now you can see for yourself that he's mine and back off. I let you have that photo session, but that's it, and make no mistake, those pictures are going suspiciously missing the minute they come in."

Tae strode toward the door, and Alise stumbled back as if she thought Tae was about to attack her. Tae put a hand on the doorknob. "Do whatever makes you happy, girlfriend. I don't give a fat rat's ass."

She swung the door open and ran smack into Daniel. His hands came up to steady her when she would have toppled backward. "I'm sorry, Tae. I didn't…" He glanced over her shoulder and must have spotted his wife. Worry creased his brow. "What's going on?"

Tae wiggled out of his hold and stepped away. "Nothing. I'm leaving. Congratulations, Daniel."

"Wait. Tae, you can't leave. The reception is about to start."

Words trembled on her lips to tell him to kiss her ass for claiming he had broken up with her and she chased after him, but she bit her tongue. She saw the disgust on Alise's face and wanted to stay just to piss her off, but she would not be accused of chasing a married man on his wedding day. "I'm sorry, Daniel, I—"

"Never meant to pull the happy couple from their guests?"

Jax's hands dropped on her shoulders, and he squeezed gently and drew her back to his chest. She tensed. "You two get back in there. We'll join you in a minute. Promise."

Daniel hesitated, looking at her rather than his wife, and then he nodded and spun to face Alise. He held out his hand to her. "Come on, sweetheart. Your Aunt Helena has an early flight, so she wanted to present us with her gift early."

Alise frowned. "That's why I told them they should come the whole weekend and leave Monday! They're ruining everything, Danny. If Aunt Helena leaves, I'm never speaking to her again."

Daniel made soothing noises and led Alise down the hall. Tae watched them go in disbelief. "Wow, mature."

"Isn't she?" Jax chuckled.

Tae shook his hands off her shoulders and rounded on him. "Why did you stop me? She cornered me in that room and accused me of chasing after Daniel. I don't need the drama, Jax. I'm leaving before I say something I'll regret."

"Say or do?"

She blinked at him. "I came. I supported him."

"If you leave now, you're only proving what she said is true."

"No one who knows me believes that."

"You're right."

Tae fell silent. She fought with a conviction to leave. Why were they even putting her into this position? One part of her felt like Jax was angry and he wanted her to stay to torture her, but he had no reason to feel that way. Not unless he didn't like that she'd snuck out in the middle of the night. What about Daniel?

Jax seemed to read her mind. "He wants to think you're okay."

She frowned. "Why wouldn't I be?"

His brows rose, and he stuck his hands in his pockets shrugging. "True. Why wouldn't you be?"

She should run for her life, but she said, "I'll stay."

❂

The reception room burst at the seams with people who had attended the wedding and a few others who hadn't. Tae sat at a table near the back, having switched out her name card from its position in a spot too close to the head table. She'd walked away from Jax after their conversation in the hall, and he didn't follow. Later, he strode in and took his seat at the head table. A short while after that, Daniel and Alise Elliott were introduced to the guests, and everyone clapped and cheered. Tae's stomach cramped. She stood and excused herself to use the bathroom. Since the reception had started, the facilities were empty, and she sighed in relief.

Standing at the sink and wetting a paper towel, she examined her face. Was she happy? Back then, all she thought about was advancing at work, progressing until she moved up from proofreader at the magazine to full-fledged editor. That goal had consumed her, and there hadn't been room for anything else. Six months ago, she obtained her goal, and she loved her job, which was why she almost never took time off.

She thought of Alise. Daniel had told her his wife worked as a customer service rep at a vehicle advertising company. If Tae knew Daniel, she imagined Alise would be pregnant before the year was out. Daniel wasn't exactly the kind of man who wanted his wife barefoot and pregnant, but he bordered on it. *Poor Alise.* Tae grinned at her reflection and dabbed her forehead with the tissue before tossing it in the trash. She left the ladies room and returned to the reception just in time to miss the newlyweds leaving her table.

"Oh, dear, you missed them." Susan Somebody, her companion to the immediate right, had identified herself as a distant cousin. Tae's mind had wandered at the part where she indicated whether she meant Daniel or Alise.

"No worries." Tae grabbed the woman's hand when she would have flagged down Daniel a few tables away. "I'll catch them later."

The older woman seemed disappointed and a little miffed at Tae. She turned to the person on the other side of her and started up a conversation about the beauty of the ceremony and how she believed Daniel and Alise were destined to be together for all eternity.

Tae lowered her lashes and toyed with her glass of water while she followed Daniel's progress. He looked so good in his finery, so quietly confident, yet friendly. By comparison, Alise spoke too loud and commanded attention at each table, growing irritable if anyone focused too long on Daniel rather than her. Soon they climbed the elevated platform to the head table, and Alise proceeded to hold court like a queen. Her mini wedding dress showed off her best asset, her legs, and from the glassiness of her eyes, Tae guessed she'd drunk too much champagne. Now that she had a ring on her finger, she didn't cling constantly to Daniel's arm, or maybe her words to Tae earlier made her feel safe. *More power to her.* In fact, Alise showered more attention on the older man next to her, who Tae understood to be her mother's boyfriend and not Alise's father. Alise's mother sat on the opposite side to this gentleman, a silent statue.

"Don't they make a lovely couple?" Susan said, deciding to give Tae another chance.

"Yes, they do," Tae agreed.

Susan chattered away, and Tae let her gaze wander to Jax. While she watched him, Jax stood and held up his glass. Tae realized servers had come around and provided everyone with champagne. She raised her own along with everyone else, and Jax started his speech. His deep voice rumbled over the audience, pitched to reach her in the back. He had dressed in a dark tux and crisp maroon shirt, with matching handkerchief. His bearing made ghosts of all the groomsmen. As she raised her glass to her lips following Jax's lead, she noticed a lock of hair fall onto his forehead. A memory flashed through her mind, of her running her fingers through his hair last night while he wore her body out. She choked on the sip of champagne and pounded her chest.

"Are you okay, dear?" Susan asked.

Eyes watering, Tae forced a smile. "I'm fine. Thank you." She peered back at Jax and found him watching her, his expression unreadable. The woman beside him, the maid of honor whose name Tae promptly forgot when she was introduced, grabbed his arm and leaned forward to show off her cleavage. She said something to Jax, and he allowed himself to be distracted by her. Of course. That was Jax. No one woman could keep his attention.

The evening wore on, and Tae made the best of it. She managed to find interesting topics of conversations with Susan and discovered the baked chicken, her choice for dinner, turned out to be delicious. Afterward, the dancing began, and when Daniel took Alise into his arms, she slipped away, went to her room to pack, and checked out of the hotel. The trip home included a stop at the grocery store for a big box of Frosted Flakes, tissues, and a DVD that no one had ever heard of from the magazine aisle.

Chapter Six

Eight weeks later…

"*No, no, no, no!*" Tae texted. "*This can't be happening, Zerita, and why aren't you here? I don't know what I'm going to do.*"

"*You're not going to make any rash decisions.*"

"*You don't understand.*"

Tae studied the stick again as she'd done a million times before. Nothing had changed. The evil device still read positive. She threw it across the bathroom, and it landed behind the toilet. Her cell phone buzzed, but she ignored it and set her head down on her arm as she leaned on the sink. Nausea rolled her stomach, an occurrence that had been happening too often lately. That along with the fact that she hadn't seen her damn period for a couple months had forced her to come out of denial and go get a pregnancy test. Now the truth stared her in the face, or it did before she slung it away.

Her cell phone buzzed twice more, and she reached for it.

"*Tae, I'm going to get out of this meeting as soon as I can. Promise me you won't be reckless.*"

"*Apparently, I've already been reckless.*"

"*Okay, we'll have the pity party a few more hours, and then that's it.*"

Despite her dark mood, Tae laughed. Leave it to Zerita not to bite her tongue.

"I deserve my pity party. My life is over."

"Dramatic much?"

Tears filled Tae's eyes, and she swiped them away. Her friend attended an out of town meeting for the writers of her magazine, so of course Tae would learn of her pregnancy at the worst possible time. She set the phone down and turned on the faucet to wash her hands and then splash water on her face. The cool liquid did nothing to lower her temperature or restore her mood. She turned from the sink and dried her hands, then headed for the kitchen. In her cabinet sat two big boxes of cereal, but corn flakes would not fix this issue.

Ice cream. She frowned, wondering at the sudden craving, not being a big ice-cream eater. Still, right now she wanted a turtle waffle bowl sundae with a chocolate-dipped cone, pecans, and caramel syrup. Making it herself was out of the question because it meant going to the grocery store to first buy the ingredients and then preparing the dessert. No, she needed a shop with the treat on the menu. None were nearby. Come to think of it, there was a Dairy Queen in South Park she could go to. The twenty-minute drive would be worth it to drown her sorrows in sugary goodness.

Halfway to the ice cream shop, Tae's craving switched to cheesecake, and she grumbled her way to South Park mall to the restaurant with the best cheesecake to be had. She found a parking space in the busy lot and strode into the restaurant and ordered two slices of the red-velvet cheesecake. Since the day mocked her with its warm sunshine, she took her treat outside and stuffed bite after bite of the creaminess into her mouth.

"PMSing?" came the amused comment.

Tae froze, fork halfway to her mouth. She turned slowly and looked up. Of all people, Daniel stood smiling over her and blocking out the sun. She'd forgotten how sometimes when she was PMSing, Daniel drove her to the mall or to Dairy Queen to get something sweet. She'd made a poor choice coming over this way, nearer to where he lived, and the thought that maybe she'd done so on purpose made the decision worse. Her appetite disappeared in a blink, and she sat up straighter in her chair, placing her fork down on the table. "Shouldn't you be on your honeymoon?"

He chuckled and sat down in the chair next to her. "We've been back a while. Can't stay on vacation forever."

What had she been thinking? The wedding took place two months ago. She'd been busy incubating Jax's baby. At the thought, her mood plummeted even more. Daniel reached out and covered her hand. Her fingers spasmed beneath his, and she pulled them free to clutch in her lap.

"What's wrong, Tae?"

She closed the lid on the cheesecake and stuffed the container in the bag along with the other slice. "Nothing. I'm great. How's married life treating you?"

Concern wrinkled the spot between his eyebrows. Her heart stirred. She suppressed the sensation and looked away, but Daniel wouldn't be put off.

"Something's upsetting you. Tell me about it."

Why the hell did he have to be so understanding? "I said it's nothing." She glanced at her phone, but she hadn't heard from Zerita since last they texted. Even if she wanted to talk to someone other than her best friend, the last person it would be was Daniel. If anything she should tell Jax first.

She shoved her chair back and dropped her head onto her folded arms. The mere thought of telling him sent her mind spinning, and her stomach tied itself in knots. Daniel touched her head and stroked her hair. He didn't ask again, but just the act of doing so loosened her lips.

"I'm pregnant," she muttered.

He leaned closer so she felt his breath on her arm. "What was that? I think you said…" He gasped. "Octavia, did you say you're—"

"Pregnant," she repeated in misery. Now that he knew, she sat up and looked into his eyes. Shock reflected back at her, and something else too. Betrayal? He had no right to feel that way. "It was an accident. I mean, I never meant…"

"Who is he?" Daniel demanded. "Do I know him?"

Do you ever. "It doesn't matter."

Daniel banged his fist on the table, and several people turned their way. He hitched his shoulders and calmed down, but the frown never left his face. "So he's some deadbeat who thought he could use your body and not deal with the consequences? Give me a name, Tae, and I'll make him regret the day he was born!"

On some level, she loved his protectiveness of her, but she wasn't some stupid woman who would cover for a dumbass loser who didn't deserve it. Besides that, Daniel knew her better. "I don't need you to stick up for me, Daniel. I can take care of it."

His eyes widened. "You're not getting an abortion!"

"Seriously? Tell the world, why don't you."

He pushed fingers through his hair, disordering it, a testament to his frustration. Unlike Jax, who looked hot as hell with tussled hair, a circumstance that happened because he didn't pay attention to messing it up, Daniel liked his in perfect order. "Sorry. Listen, I can help you."

"Help me what?" She put a hand on her hip. "Did you forget you have a wife, Daniel? What are you going to help me do exactly?"

"Figure this thing out."

She stood and gathered her bag. "I don't need your help, but thanks. I shouldn't even have come over to this side of town. Just like I ran into you, I could have run into anyone." She clamped her teeth together so fast her jaw hurt, but the blunder had already slipped out. Daniel's expression shifted from curiosity to shock and then to anger. She swung away from him and started to walk away, but he caught her arm and turned her back to face him.

"Tell me the truth," he demanded, clutching her arms.

She winced. "You're hurting me, Daniel." He refused to let go no matter how she struggled.

"Tell me, Octavia!" He drew her closer to his chest, and she managed to bring her hands up before her breasts flattened against him. "Is it Jax's baby?"

She swallowed. Refusing to answer would keep her there all day. Besides, he had already figured it out because of her mistake. She should have let him believe it was some loser, but she wasn't in the habit of lying and playing games with people, especially not Daniel.

"Yes. Happy now?"

"Not by a long shot! I can't believe you would sleep with my best friend."

When he put it like that, he made her sound like a slut, and she refused to apologize. She wiggled from his hold. "Who I choose to sleep with is none of your business. Please do me the favor of not saying anything to Jax."

Disbelief echoed in his voice. "You're not going to tell him?"

"I will in my time, not yours. Promise, Daniel."

He stared at her for a few minutes.

"*Daniel*."

"You have my word."

She nodded and spun to walk away. All the while her legs quivered and her stomach heaved. When she reached her car, she unlocked it, slung the door wide, and tossed the unwanted cheesecake to the passenger seat. Somehow, it felt like things had gone from bad to worse in a matter of hours.

❋

Tae bent to heft a huge basket of laundry and then froze. She bit her lip wondering. If she remembered correctly from her sisters' pregnancies, it was not a good idea to lift anything too heavy. She hadn't yet decided whether she would keep the baby, but to be on the safe side, she dragged the basket instead. Was that also too much strain?

In the kitchen, she sorted the whites from the colors and loaded her tiny washing machine. She had to do several loads because of the basin's size. If she had a baby, the labor would increase. On top of the laundry, she would need more space as her apartment accommodated her but would never be sufficient for a child. She chewed her lip thinking about her budget. The new position came with a raise, but not that much, especially with her sister calling every month for financial help because of this and that reason. Things would have to change.

Wait, does that mean I'm keeping it?

She glanced down at her stomach, soft and somewhat round, but that was because of her extra pounds to start with. She hadn't noticed any weight gain yet. While she tried to imagine her stomach protruding at nine months, her cell phone rang. "That better be Zerita."

She punched the button without consciously registering the name. The deep familiar voice took her by surprise. "I hear congratulations are in order."

Tae blinked at the stark bitterness and unmistakable anger. "What?"

"You're pregnant," he growled across the line.

Tae dropped the shirt she'd pulled out of the basket and sank to the floor next to it. Her breath caught in her throat, and her eyes burned. She shut them, sagging forward, trying to think what to say to him. Daniel had claimed she had his word, but he lied, the bastard. Zerita certainly hadn't spilled her news—one because she was still trapped in her meetings, and two, she just wouldn't betray Tae's trust. Tae had thought Daniel wouldn't either, but she was wrong.

"Nothing to say?" Jax demanded. Odd, she had rarely seen Jax angry, and it had never been aimed at her. Not that she'd ever done anything to piss him off. She knew he was mad now because he had to hear about the pregnancy from someone else.

She switched the cell phone from one hand to the other and rubbed a clammy palm over her pant leg. The movement drew her attention to the waistband of said pants, and she wondered how long she would fit into them.

"So Daniel told you," she said at last.

He swore. "At least you had the decency to tell him."

Tae frowned. "Okay, lose the attitude, Jax. Now you know! I didn't go about all this the right way, but I expected Daniel to keep my secret more than a freaking day to give me time to get my head on straight."

"Let's get *this* straight. My buddy did not betray your trust."

All kinds of insinuations permeated his words, as if she were the one to betray trust. Like she'd spread her legs and knocked herself up, all while disappointing the great Jaxon Hart, who had nothing to do with it. "Then why don't you tell me how you knew then?"

"Alise."

Tae's jaw fell open. "Daniel told Alise?"

"Of course not! You and Daniel were too busy arguing on the street to realize Alise was there. She heard everything, and she came to me devastated."

Tae blinked. Why would Alise be devastated? Tae's pregnancy had nothing to do with the woman. Did her drive to be the center of attention in Daniel's world make her upset that Tae had confided in him? The possibility wasn't unreasonable. No woman wanted another woman to use her husband as a confidant. At the realization, guilt rolled over Tae, and she rubbed a hand across her forehead, which had begun to pound.

"I'm—" she began.

"You're what?" he interrupted. "Sorry for trying to destroy a marriage?"

"Excuse you?"

"I knew you still loved him, but I never thought you would seduce him after he married Alise. Guess I had you pegged wrong, didn't I? How many times was it before it took?"

Dawning realization hit Tae hard. Alise hadn't heard everything like she claimed. She'd only heard enough to know Tae was pregnant, and she had jumped to the conclusion the baby was Daniel's. That didn't even touch on Jax's opinion of Tae.

She squeezed the cell phone in her hand until she heard a crack and hoped it was the cheap case and not the phone itself. "Why don't you come out and say it, Jax? I mean you're accusing me of being a scheming ho, aren't you? Like I got pregnant to try to get Daniel back? Never mind that I haven't tried anything in the last three years or that we barely saw each other more than a couple times a month."

"A lot changes when a man is about to become unavailable."

"You know what? Fuck you!" She took the phone away from her ear and stabbed the Disconnect button. A few minutes passed while she sobbed into a T-shirt, and then she scrubbed her face and dialed Daniel. He answered on the first ring, which did nothing for her guilt. "Daniel, have you talked to Alise today?"

"Ah, this morning when I left for the office," he said, confusion obvious. "Why?"

"She thinks my baby is yours."

"What?"

Something smashed, and Daniel dropped the phone. She waited for him to get control of it, but more muffled sounds came over the line, along with Daniel's curses.

"Daniel, are you there?"

"Sorry, I'm here. Tell me why my wife would think I got you pregnant."

She sighed and explained how Alise had overheard part of their conversation. "So at some point, she was there, and she went running to Jax to tell him."

"Damn it. I have to call her. No, I'm leaving work. Tae, how are you? Jax take the news fine?"

"He thinks the baby is yours."

"I get that, but you straightened him out?"

She fell silent.

"Octavia?"

"He accused me of being a slut."

"I will kill him."

She smiled. "Don't worry about it. I'll tell him the truth when I'm ready. Right now, I just need to get my head together. Please, Daniel, a little longer. You should get things straight with Alise, but I'd rather wait as far as Jax. I hope you understand."

"It's not my decision. I said I would keep your secret, and I will. I hope you'll fix this soon, Tae. Personally, I think Jax deserves to know he's going to be a father. It's the most amazing gift a woman could ever give a man."

Rip out my heart and stomp it, why don't you?

"Everyone knows how you feel about having a family."

"And everyone knows you don't want a family," he shot back.

The pain in her head grew. "It's not that I don't. You wouldn't understand. I grew up with a full house. I never had my own space, never got any privacy. Hell, my family still tugs at me as much as they can, so yes, I wanted a lifestyle where it was just me, and I don't have to feel bad about that."

"You're right. You don't, but that all changed the moment you got pregnant. Tae, you have to do what's best for the child."

"Yeah, well I don't have to decide today! I have to go. I hope everything works out with Alise." She disconnected the call before he could say more.

For the rest of the day, Tae did laundry and cleaned up her apartment. All the while, she mulled Daniel's words in her head as well as her own. Was she being selfish and immature, thinking of her space, her peace, her carefully constructed lifestyle? One could look at the other side and consider she was not right for motherhood with her attitude, and a baby might be better off either unborn or given up for adoption. The word adoption pulled her up short. She'd not thought of that before now. Could she even do it, go through nine months of pregnancy only to sign the baby over to someone else?

What about Jax? She knew Daniel longed for a family. They had discussed at length the subject when they dated. Daniel had wanted to marry her and to have kids right away. He'd suggested she stop work to care for their children, and when she told him he must be out of his mind, he'd "conceded" to her staying home until the children were five and then working part-time. Again she'd let him know he would not decide whether she worked or not. He apparently didn't get how firm her conviction was because he'd soon after asked her to marry him. While she loved him with all her heart at the time, she had turned him down, knowing they weren't right for each other. Daniel was a good man, sweet and attentive, but he needed a woman who was content to be a housewife and a mother. She was not the one.

On the other hand, she had no idea what Jax felt about kids or getting married. He'd come off as content jumping from woman to woman, and really since he wouldn't carry the baby, his lifestyle needn't change. Did he want kids? Would he want to be involved now that they'd produced a child?

After the chores were all done, Tae sat down at her desk in her home office and opened her checkbook. She looked at the current balance and sighed. Somewhere in her drawer was the statement for her savings account—almost nil. She rubbed fingers over her temple and scanned the office, what the rental agent had called a "den." A joke if she'd ever heard one, the den looked more like a walk-in closet, a tiny one, but she had fitted it with a desk and chair, all that could squeeze in without her feeling claustrophobic. Even examining the room now, she knew converting it into a nursery would not work. Closing the door would make it seem like she'd shut her baby into a closet. A tight pain squeezed her chest, and she frowned down at her belly.

"My baby?"

Ah hell, I'm going to keep it. Now what?

Chapter Seven

Tae stepped out of the shower and dried off with a towel. Doing so made her think of bathing her baby. How did one know if the temperature was too hot or too cool? Did she go by her own feelings, or was baby's skin more sensitive to heat? Grumbling her frustration, she left the bathroom and lotioned her body, then slipped into a pair of jeans and a simple blouse. She wondered if she should wear a dress instead and then remembered she'd probably have to remove all her clothing anyway and put on one of those hospital gowns. Another grumble escaped. She hated going to the doctor, and now being pregnant, she'd have to go a billion times.

While she pulled on a sock, the doorbell rang, and she paused, wondering who it was. She strode into the living room and checked the peephole. Her heart stuttered at sight of Daniel, and she worked to calm down before she opened the door. "Daniel, what are you doing here?"

"I'm here for you."

Her brows rose and mouth fell open before she snapped out of it. "What do you mean you're here for me?"

He pushed past her into the apartment, and she stood there looking after him.

"Close the door, Tae." He scanned her from head to foot and grinned at her feet. "Lose a sock?"

"No, I was in the middle of getting dressed. I have my first doctor's appointment in about an hour." She folded her arms over her chest. "You didn't answer my question. What are you doing here?"

"Actually, I did," he countered. The cool attitude rivaled her agitated one until she wanted to choke the man. When she waited for more, he went on. "I've decided to support you with the baby, and it looks like I have great timing. I'll go with you for your doctor's visit."

"I think you forgot you're married. You need to be 'supporting' your wife."

She made air quotes to emphasize her words, but at her statement, the calm self-assurance in Daniel's expression transformed first to sadness and then to anger. His lips compressed, and his eyebrows crashed low over his eyes. Tae dreaded what that meant. She started to prompt him to explain the reaction but didn't need to.

"Even though I told Alise I did not father your baby, she still packed and went to her mother's."

"No!" Tae slapped a hand over her mouth. Tears sprung to her eyes and fell down her cheeks. "I'm so sorry, Daniel. This is my fault."

He drew her into his arms and stroked her hair. "No, it's not. You did nothing wrong, and if my marriage is so flimsy a misunderstanding can destroy it, then you were right. Alise is not for me."

She wrenched from his hold. "You're not throwing it away just like that. You need to fight for her, Daniel. I'm going to call her and explain that you and I didn't have sex, so it's impossible to even think you're the father of my baby. It's just ridiculous, and our meeting that day was just happenstance. She has to believe me."

Tae spun to go to her room to get her phone, but Daniel grabbed her arm to stop her. "Forget it."

"What do you mean forget it? You love her. I think—"

"Aren't you going to be late for your appointment?"

She glanced at the clock on the dining room wall. The metal bicycle design was so unique she'd had to buy it. Daniel was right. She didn't have much time. "Well I'll call afterward."

"No, you won't." He shuffled her toward her bedroom. "I'll handle it. Hurry up, and I'll take you."

"Daniel."

"I'm not accepting no for an answer, Tae. Finish getting dressed. I'm going with you. End of discussion." While he had been assertive, his tone remained kind. She sighed and gave in. Zerita wasn't in town, and even if she were, Tae had only been able to get a day appointment. She couldn't ask her friend to take off work with her to go to the doctor.

"How did you know I was home?"

He grinned and winked. "I have my ways."

She rolled her eyes. "Fine. I'll be ready in a minute."

Tae hurried into her bedroom and drew on her other sock, then put on shoes. She started out to the living room and had to run back to look for the notebook where she recorded the dates for her period. After making a mental note of the last two, she rejoined Daniel, and they headed out.

Tae started toward her car, but Daniel placed a hand on her lower back. "I'm parked this way." She decided not to argue and followed him to his vehicle. When they were on the road, she told him the address and studied him as he drove. One large hand gripped the steering wheel while the other rested on his thigh. A ridiculous longing came over her to lay hers atop his, but she resisted it and faced the window. Scenery raced by, but she saw none of it. Her thoughts were filled with memories of Daniel, and for some reason, his voice echoed in her head of the many times he had confessed his love. Daniel was the type of man to never hold back how he felt. She had never had to wonder or be unsure of him. That fact was one of the reasons she had loved him so much.

"Tae?"

She came to herself and looked at him. "Sorry, I was daydreaming."

"No problem." He frowned at the car ahead, which cut him off, and adjusted his speed. "I was asking if you told Jax about the baby yet."

She bit her lip. "Not yet."

"Why not, Tae?"

"Don't get onto me. I told you. I'll tell him when I'm ready."

"Tell me why you're *not* ready."

"I…"

He glanced at her, waiting, and she sighed, spreading her hands. How did she explain having him come along with her to her appointment made things worse for her rather than better? Jax had accused her of sleeping with Daniel multiple times trying to get pregnant. Of course he was wrong, but that didn't stop her from liking him here now. If she told Jax, then what? Would he want to be here, too? She'd slept with him, and it was good as hell, but she never imagined it going further, of them doing the whole domestic thing. Yet, the longer she delayed telling him the truth, the harder it became to do it. Her selfishness knew no bounds, but even realizing that didn't propel her.

"It was my fault. I should have asked him to use a condom."

Daniel winced at her candor.

"I knew I wasn't on the pill because I hadn't been with anyone for a while."

This time he looked hard at her, and she hated the hope she saw in his gaze. "So you haven't been with anyone since me...and Jax."

"I didn't say that." He didn't need to know the truth.

"I'm not going to lie, Tae." He pulled to a stop at a red light and twisted to face her. "I'd give anything for that baby to be mine."

"Don't say that!!"

"Why not?" He touched her cheek, and an overwhelming urge to lean in to the touch assailed her. She found the strength not to but moving out of reach didn't happen.

"Because you're married."

"I'm separated."

"No different. I don't get involved with married men."

"I wasn't suggesting that you do."

Embarrassed that she'd jumped to conclusions, she stared out the window and squeezed her fingers together so tight they hurt. If her hands stayed in her lap, she couldn't reach out to touch him as he did her, tempting beyond all reason.

"You're not being fair, Daniel."

"I don't mean to be a jerk."

She laughed. "You a jerk? That could never happen. Alise doesn't know what she's screwing up."

He tapped her cheek, and she turned to look at him. Her heart leaped in her chest just gazing into his eyes. "I won't lie and say I don't love you anymore, Tae. You will always be important to me. Like I said, I'd give anything to be the father of your child."

"Because you always wanted a family."

Daniel had an older brother he wasn't close to, and his parents had moved to Florida the second he turned eighteen and left him in Charlotte to fend for himself. Tae had always found it funny how kind and warm he turned out despite his past.

"Not just that," he said. "A child needs an attentive father."

He made it sound like Jax would never be. Daniel knew Jax better than she did.

"I know I'm not being fair to my friend, but I never thought I would feel like I'm competing with him for you and for your baby."

Tae swallowed. This conversation had gone way beyond what she'd intended. While hearing Daniel say he loved her gave her the greatest thrill of her life, guilt weighed on her shoulders like a boulder. Jax deserved to be allowed the chance to be a part of his baby's life, even if he didn't love her. He didn't deserve them judging him to be less than Daniel would be as a daddy.

"This isn't a competition," she said. "I'm going to tell him, and you are my friend and nothing more. I need you to be clear about that."

"Do I hear an *or* in there somewhere?"

Daniel pulled into the parking lot outside her doctor's office, so she had an excuse not to answer. When he switched off the car, she unbuckled her seat belt and stepped out of the car. She left him to follow her into the office and was soon called to go to the back.

The nurse winked and held the door for her. "Daddy can come too if you want."

Tae's steps faltered. "He's not—"

"Thanks," Daniel interrupted. "Don't mind if I do."

Tae frowned at him and placed a hand in the middle of his chest to stop him. "You can wait out here. I won't be long." Disappointment colored his face, but he didn't argue, and Tae escaped through the door. Touching Daniel and having him so close, so sweet, was more than she could handle. From now on, she would need to keep him at a distance. When the door shut, cutting him off from view, she faced the nurse. "He is a friend, and I'm pretty sure my business shouldn't be blurted out in the waiting room, especially since I haven't even had a blood test yet to confirm the home test I took. At least that's the little I read about before I came here. Am I wrong?"

Color drained from the woman's face. "I'm so sorry, Ms. Croft. You're right. Please accept my apology."

"Kate?"

Both Tae and the nurse turned in the direction of the authoritative voice. One of the doctors stood nearby, a man. Tae had never liked having a male doctor, so the times Dr. Chen wasn't available, she'd chosen to see the nurse practitioner.

"May I have a word with you in private?" the doctor said.

If possible, Kate paled even more. Now Tae panicked. "It's not a big deal, a small mistake. We're fine." Kate cast her a grateful glance, but the doctor ushered her away, and another nurse took her place. The royal treatment commenced as if she were someone of high importance. After the nurse finished taking her weight, she led Tae to a room, and every staff member on the way greeted her with smiles and other pleasantries. Not until she'd been left alone a few moments to change into a gown did she realize why. They treated her the way they did because she was in a position to sue.

Breaking a personal record, Dr. Chen appeared less than five minutes later. "How are we doing, Tae?"

"*We* are probably pregnant," she said, unhappy. "But before that, I hope I didn't get Kate into trouble. It really was no big deal."

"Let's concentrate on you." With her usual perky attitude, she ran down the plan for the current visit. "We won't discuss any visits in the future until we're sure. Now, when was your last period?"

Tae dealt with all the questions, the giving of blood, and receiving a mountain of information once it had been confirmed she was indeed pregnant. She arranged for the next office visit, at her ten-week mark for a sonogram and then returned to the waiting room to meet Daniel.

He stood up and walked toward her, causing her heart to pound out of control. "Everything okay?" he asked, and she nodded, unable to speak. "How about lunch?"

She considered coming up with an excuse, but the truth was she wanted to be with him a little longer. "I'd love to."

❧

By the time Tae returned home, it was after five. She had spent the entire day with Daniel. They had had lunch, and then at his suggestion, they had gone window shopping at Concord Mills mall. Both of them felt it was too early to begin buying baby items, but that didn't mean they couldn't peruse what was out there for babies. The more they conferred on colors and styles, clothing and furniture, the more she enjoyed herself with him. When he dropped her at her door, she couldn't help admitting at least part of her feelings.

"I wanted to thank you for today," she said, a tremor in her voice as she stared at the floor like a child.

"It was my pleasure."

She looked up at him. "No, you don't understand. I… didn't know if I wanted kids. Not that I didn't like them. It's just that I was scared, and I'm still terrified, but you made me feel a little bit excited about the baby, and I'm grateful. So thanks."

He took her hands in his, and she tried to pull away, but he held on. "Don't pull away, Tae. I promised you I would be here for you, and I will. You don't have to feel like you're alone— whether it's with emotional support or even financial, I'm going to be here."

"Hold up, cowboy." She managed to get free. "I can take care of my own child."

"I know."

She waggled a finger at him. "Get that straight."

He chuckled. "It's straight."

"Why do I feel like you'll still be offering me help?"

"Because I will."

She rolled her eyes. "Good night, Daniel."

He leaned forward without warning and kissed her cheek. A gush of sensation raced to her nether regions. "Good night," he whispered, and he strode down the stairs toward the street like he hadn't just ruined her panties with a chaste kiss. Tae ducked into her apartment, shut the door, and locked it, but no barrier could keep memories of the past from invading her mind and making her relive the pleasure of lying in Daniel's arms.

Chapter Eight

Tae was twenty-four when she started dating Daniel. At twenty-eight, he was mature and confident, but friendly and attentive. They met in a bookstore where Tae had been buying smut, and Daniel had been buying something ridiculously boring like the political economy of the mass media. When she had rounded a corner and bumped into him, both their piles of books went flying, and he joined her on the floor to gather them. His smile and those eyes had taken her breath away from the start, but the fact that he'd see what she chose to read made her consider not for the first time of giving up the paperback stuff for books for the new thing she'd heard about—an e-reader, whatever that was.

She grabbed *Big Girls Do It Better* and dropped it on his stack of books. "I think this one's yours."

He looked down and read the cover, then back up at her. At his confused blink, Tae bit the inside of her cheek and fought not to crack a smile. After a moment, he grinned, and the sunshine came out in her world. "I don't think so, but why would *you* read it?"

Now the tables were turned, and she struggled to defend her habit of devouring pieces that had little to do with her major in literature. "I…"

His hot gaze traveled from her face, to her breasts, on down to her wide hips and thighs. "You don't match the woman on the cover, but then maybe you were curious?"

Was this his way of complimenting her? Or was he saying she wasn't white like the woman on the cover, so why was she in his face? Before she could formulate an answer, he continued.

"You're a very beautiful woman and a far cry from being described as 'big.'"

Her heart almost leaped from her chest. "I think you missed my thick thighs and big booty, but thank you for the compliment."

He helped her to her feet and gathered the rest of her books. Rather than hand them over, he offered to carry them to the register for her, and Tae accepted.

Before she knew it they were dating, and she was falling desperately in love. There had been one problem at the time— she was a virgin, and while she was no little thing like he claimed, Daniel was huge both in height and build—and in his pants. The night she invited him to her apartment with a mind toward having sex, she'd been nervous as hell.

Daniel wore slacks and a button-up shirt. His blond hair was combed to perfect order, and he looked good enough to eat. In fact, the whiff of his cologne made her mouth water. The man made things worse when he touched her arm in a gentle caress, his blue eyes filled with concern.

"What's wrong, Tae? You look frightened."

She'd clutched her hands together, swallowing the lump in her throat. *Damn it, I'm twenty-four. Get a grip, Tae. Just tell him the truth.* She'd opened her mouth, but confessing her lack of experience turned out to be impossible.

Daniel's thumb caressed her bare arm. She'd worn a miniskirt and a matching blouse with spaghetti straps. The V neckline plunged low enough to tease with her ample cleavage but was still tasteful. While she dithered trying to find the courage to say something, his gaze dropped to her breasts and lingered. She'd been looking down and noticed the tent rise in his pants. This wasn't the first time, but she didn't blame him. Her panties had needed changing on too many occasions after he'd left them soaked with his kisses and his roaming hands.

"You know I love you, don't you, honey?" he said.

She melted and raised her hands to his waist. Daniel drew her closer so she rested her head against his chest. "I know. I love you, too."

He leaned back and lifted her chin. "We don't have to do this. I can wait."

She tried striking a sassy pose. "Please, I invited you, remember?"

"And you're a virgin."

Her world crumbled. "You knew?"

"Of course."

Panic tightened her throat so she had to force words out. "Because of my kisses?"

His brows creased. "Your kisses bring me to my knees. No other woman has tasted as good as you. No, I know because of your fear and how many times we've been at this point and you've backed off with an excuse. If it was just that you wanted to be sure it wouldn't be a one-night stand, I think you would have given in ages ago."

She groaned. "I'm sorry, Daniel. I really do want you, but I don't know why all this time I haven't found the one I wanted to give my virginity to. Not until I met you. I don't want to lose you."

He grasped both her arms and gave her a small shake. "You are not going to let me make love to you because you're scared to lose me! With that this plan is canceled. Go get your shoes. We'll go bowling or something or to a movie."

"But we were going to—"

He gazed at her breasts again and dropped his hands to his sides as if she'd burned him. When he turned his back, it hurt her, but she got it. That decision was what did it for her. Daniel was willing to suffer blue balls rather than take her for the wrong reasons.

"Hurry up, *please*."

"Okay." She smiled behind his back and spun away to head to her room. Once there, she began stripping out of her clothes. She tossed the tank on the floor and unbuttoned the skirt. In her bra and panties, she was about to call him, but changed her mind. If Daniel only saw her underwear, he might be able to resist. She needed to be naked. The panties hit the chair, followed by the bra. She bent in half trying not to hyperventilate, but blood rushed to her head instead.

"Tae, honey?" Daniel called.

She squeaked and darted across the room, farthest from the door. A glimpse of herself in the full-length mirror brought her to a stop, and she examined her body. Not too bad, thick thighs but not dimply. A big butt appealed to a lot of men. She liked her boobs. They hung just right, and her nipples puckered from being uncovered.

Tae climbed on the bed and struck a pose, turned on her side, a hand on her hip, and one leg bent. Maybe she should get some water and go to the bathroom.

"Tae!"

Her heart stopped. Daniel stood in the doorway staring at her. Boy did she hope he really loved her, because he'd confessed he hadn't dated a black woman, and he was in for a surprise when he got a load of her dark pussy. She waited for him to speak, but he had frozen like a statue.

"Well?" she demanded. "Do you like me or not?"

He shook his head, and she thought she'd sink through the bed and down through the floor. He left the doorway and approached with an unsteady gait. "You've got to be sure, Tae, because you look so good, I can't help myself. I have to have you. I don't like you. I *love* you, and there is no way we're bowling tonight!"

She rolled onto her back and tossed an arm over her eyes. The bed sank down as he climbed onto it. She gasped. Daniel's fingers curled around one ankle, and he gave it a tug, spreading her legs. Her pussy opened to him. She dared to take a peek at his reaction. The man appeared mesmerized. He licked his lips and slid his hand up her leg to her thigh. A nudge of his knuckles widened her legs even more.

"Will the come taste the same?" he wondered aloud.

She panted. "I-I don't know."

"I have to find out." He started to jerk at his shirt buttons but stopped himself and then began undoing each of them with trembling fingers. All the while, he didn't take his eyes off her. She felt like a meal laid out just for him, and it turned her on big time. He placed his clothes on the chair where she'd tossed her underwear earlier. His clothes were laid out neatly, and she would have laughed at the difference between them, but nerves kept her silent.

Daniel returned to the bed and climbed between her legs. He paused every so often to kiss her skin and caress it. At her apex, he leaned down and breathed deep. A shudder shook her from head to toe.

His gaze met hers. "This is my first time too in a sense. We'll learn each other. Tae, I don't want you be afraid. I promise I won't hurt you. I'll take my time, and you tell me if there's anything you don't like. I'll stop."

The gentle assertion soothed her raw nerves, but they jangled up again in a different way when he lowered his mouth between her legs to lave her slit. She squirmed and moaned. He rested tender hands on her thighs, not holding her down but comforting her.

"Daniel."

"Easy, baby. It's okay. I'm going to take it slow."

He used his thumbs to part her folds and teased the tip of her clit with his tongue. She cried out and moaned, unable to keep her hips from rising off the bed. A man may never have penetrated her, but she knew how to bring herself to orgasm. The pleasure from her own fingers did not compare to the bliss from Daniel's hungry mouth. He sucked her clit into his mouth, and a powerful orgasm descended within seconds. She touched his shoulders, whether to push him back or draw him closer, she didn't know. In the end, she closed her thighs, trapping him between them and arched her hips to ride his face. Daniel sucked and sucked, holding a rhythm that drove her wild. She whimpered his name. The orgasm took control. The second she let go, he replaced his lips with his thumb and massaged her clit while he licked her flowing juices.

The entire time Daniel feasted on her pussy, he made sure not to push his tongue too far past her lips. Still, he lapped up every drop of her come and then climbed up the bed to lie beside her. Tae curled into his arms, feeling his hard cock between them.

"I want to please you," she said.

"Have you ever given a man head before?"

She considered saying yes and then doing her best, but she couldn't lie to him. "No, I thought if I did that, it would lead to more."

"Then we'll save it for later. First, I'm going to make you fully mine."

Her eyes widened. She pressed a hand to his bare chest, and tingles of awareness raced up and down her fingers to her arms.

Desire kept her from telling him no, but fear balled the muscles in her belly to knots. She swallowed, trying to wet an arid throat. Funny all the wetness lay in her eyes as she tried not to cry. *What a scaredy cat. Just do it. You want him.*

Daniel hovered over her with kind eyes. He raised her hand from his chest and kissed her fingers. "Do you want me to stop?"

"N-No." She cursed herself for showing her fear. "I want this." To demonstrate, she pulled from his grasp and ran her hand down his chest to his abs. At first she watched her exploration, loving the sight of his body, so hard and sexy. His tanned skin made her weak in the knees and wet between the legs. She'd seen him naked before when she was at his house and he'd stepped from the shower, not even worried about her getting a look. Maybe he'd wanted her to. That's how she knew his cock was big. Now as she touched his body, she lost the nerve to look at his shaft while she reached for it. Daniel chuckled, and she frowned at him.

"It's not funny."

"Aw." He grinned, making her heart beat faster. "No, it's not." He wrapped his fingers around hers and taught her how to stroke him. They started at the bottom and slid up, then down again. He shut his eyes and tilted his head back. In fascination, she watched, thrilled that she made him feel this good.

His cock twitched under her palm, and she gave it a tug. Daniel stilled her hand. "Easy."

Her eyes widened. "I'm sorry. Did I hurt you?"

"No." He raised her chin and kissed her, then pushed her back so she lay flat on the bed. He leaned over her, staring into her eyes. His muscular arm seemed to block out half the room when he reached to brush her hair from her face. "I will teach you everything you need to know to please me, but first…"

His fingers found her heat, and she started to look down, but he clicked with his tongue.

"No, baby, look at me."

She held onto his arms, shaking, and he parted her lips to slip one finger inside. Her pussy ached. Daniel waited until her hold eased, and then he pushed in a second finger. He stroked deep into her box and then pulled out, his digits coated with her juices. Her breaths came heavy and fast. She wanted to shut her eyes, but she forced herself to keep looking at him. The love reflected in the blue depths helped her to relax a little, and he nodded his approval.

"Hold on. I'm going to put on a condom. Just relax. It'll be okay."

She loved him more and more seeing his concern for her, and she waited as calm as she cold while he tore open the packet he'd fished from his pants pocket. The magnum-sized condom rolled onto his shaft, and Daniel positioned himself between her legs. Tae squeezed her eyes shut and balled her hands into fists at her sides.

"I shouldn't have waited so long. I shouldn't have waited. I shouldn't have…" she chanted.

"Hey." Daniel's voice came from just above her, and she opened her eyes. The same man she'd loved for months stretched above her. While she knew from the stiffness of his cock he must want her bad, he maintained control and waited for her. She wasn't being fair. He brought her to an orgasm, and she wanted to please him.

She uncurled her fingers and stroked his cheek. Leaning up, she kissed his lips and pushed her tongue into his mouth. He responded, teasing the tip of her tongue with his until they deepened the kiss. When she raised her knees, he settled on top of her, and she drew in a sharp breath as his cock pierced her entrance, expanding the cramped opening and making her cry out in pain.

"I'm sorry, baby. I'm so sorry," he murmured around kisses on her lips. His hands shifted to her hips, and he held still while she got used to the feeling of him deep inside her. Her pussy hurt like hell, but it felt good too, better than she imagined it could the first time. "I'm going to push in farther. Hold on. I'll make you feel good soon."

She clutched his shoulders, digging her fingernails into his skin without meaning to and unable to stop. "It already feels good, Daniel. Give me everything. I want all of you."

He drove in deeper, until his pelvis bumped hers, and Tae encircled his neck with her arms. Her head spun with the pleasure that increased as the pain diminished. Daniel placed his hand under her ass and pushed her up toward him. The angle made his cock surge into her heat at a different angle, and she gasped at the change in sensation. Her jaw went slack, and she shut her eyes. He drove in slow and gentle, and then withdrew only to invade her pussy again. She wrapped her legs around his waist and rested her heels on his ass.

"Again," she begged. "Don't stop. Please don't stop."

"I'm not going to quit until we both come," he promised, and she gave herself to him, body and soul.

When Daniel reached the end of his control, he plunged into her heat and stilled. She looked up at him, marveling at the expression of bliss. His forehead dropped, and he buried his face in the pillow beside her. His entire body jerked, and he lay heavy on top of her. Then she felt it, an odd sensation, heat, and pulsing as he pumped his seed into the condom. Tae whooped in silence. She'd done it. She'd made her man come, and just watching him had sent her lust so high, all she had to do was wiggle her hips while Daniel was still inside her to come a second time. The orgasm consumed her, tightening her core muscles and making her moan and whisper his name. When the sensations eased, Daniel pulled out and lay at her side. He drew her gently into his arms, and Tae drifted off to sleep, sore but content.

Chapter Nine

Tae heard the doorbell ringing, but she couldn't roll off the couch onto the floor to crawl across the floor. *Roll* and *crawl* were the operative words since she'd collapsed where she lay not an hour ago. A marathon of vomiting in the bathroom had led to her present position. How could this happen anyway? From all she'd heard and from its freaking name "morning sickness" should happen in the morning. Besides that, wasn't it too early? She'd thought to check the literature her doctor had given her, but she forgot it in her purse, which happened to be in the bedroom.

The doorbell rang again, and she moaned in agony. A heavy banging started, and then she heard Jax shouting through the door. "I know you're in there, Tae. Open up."

For real?

She rolled to her knees on the side of the couch and managed to use the coffee table to stand up. After what felt like years, she reached the front door and undid the locks. Peeking out at Jax, she studied his form. He looked the same, normal, unaffected by this damn sickness, and he'd done it to her. Life wasn't fair.

"What are you doing here, Jax? Come to call me more names?"

"I came to apologize."

She blinked. He brought the hand from behind his back that she hadn't noticed and presented her with flowers, a beautiful array of red tulips and blue irises. The sweet scent stirred her stomach, and she backed away, slapping a hand over her mouth. Alarm registered in Jax's expression.

"Damn, I didn't realize." He looked left and right, spinning this way and that. If she weren't feeling so bad, she would have laughed. At last he jogged the flowers over to her neighbor's place, yanked the card free, and plunked them down to the side of the door. Then he hurried back to her. "Let me help you to the bathroom."

She raised a hand, but he ignored it and roughly jerked her into his arms to carry her down the hall. When they reached the bathroom, he set her on her feet and lifted the lid to the toilet. Next thing she knew, he sat before the commode with her on his lap and him holding her hair in one hand.

"Go," he said, and she laughed.

"Is that a command, sir?"

"I mean it's okay to let loose."

She shook her head and found it to be a mistake. For want of energy to do anything else, she laid her head on his shoulder. "It's past now. I don't have anything left in my stomach."

Jax touched her face with calloused hands, so unlike Daniel's, which were soft. Jax stood, carrying her with him and walked from the bathroom to the living room. He laid her down on the couch and took a spot on the loveseat not far away. She breathed a sigh of relief because sitting on his lap had not done anything for her equilibrium.

"Tae."

"Hm?" she murmured.

"You reek."

Her eyes popped open, and she pushed herself to her elbows. "I just told you I was sick. No one invited you to stay. If I offend your nose, you can get out."

She glared at him, but her lower lip trembled. Was this the emotional roller coaster she remembered her sister telling her about when she was pregnant? Tae hadn't spent much time with Janita or Sasha, so she wasn't sure. Lack of sleep could do it, too.

He stood up, and she folded her arms on the couch and put her head face down on them. Good riddance. She didn't need him or anyone else either. His footsteps receded, but she never heard the door open and close. Instead the bathroom faucet came on, and she heard clunking around, sounds she identified with the hall closet. The sound the water made changed, and she guessed Jax filled a container with water. If he was thirsty, why didn't he go to the kitchen and use the dispenser in the refrigerator door? For that matter, what the hell did he use to get the water?

She started to sit up when she heard him coming back. He hurried over to her, water sloshing above the side of the basin he carried. Tae ground her teeth and said nothing at wet splotches on the carpet. Jax dropped to his knees beside her, and a whiff of strawberry rose from the sudsy water. He must have squeezed in her bath gel. When he dipped a washcloth into the water, she drew back.

"What are you going to do with that?"

"Wash you."

"Dude, seriously? I'll brush my teeth and gargle, okay?" She tried to sit up, but dizziness assailed her, and she fell back down. Jax caught her and righted her on the couch.

"Lie still."

"I don't need your help, Jax. Every woman goes through this when they're pregnant," she lied, having no clue if her statement was true. "I can deal with it."

He ignored her protests and pulled his jacket from his shoulders. That's when she noticed the gun. Her heart skittered and then beat faster. Jax followed her line of sight, and looked down at himself. "Damn, sorry about that. I came here from a job."

"You had to carry a gun?"

"I often carry one when I'm working. I have a license to carry a concealed weapon."

"That seems dangerous."

"It can be. Now, forget about the gun. I'll take the holster off. Just relax."

She kept looking until he'd divested himself of the weapon and set it on the coffee table. "I said I don't need help."

He reached out to unbutton her blouse. She smacked his hands. He frowned. "We can do this the easy way or the hard way."

"Are you going to hit me over the head?"

"No, but I can pin you down."

"You'd like that!"

"Tae, I'm here to help you. I know you don't want it, but the last I spoke with Daniel, he decided to work on his marriage."

She gasped. The words cut. Not that she thought Daniel should stay by her and ignore is own wife, but she had enjoyed her time with him the other day. Even if she never wanted a family, the experience of having Daniel visiting the doctor's office with her and shopping for the baby with her was kind of nice. But Daniel didn't have the right to be here. Jax did, and she resented him for it.

"I'm not an invalid," she said.

"How long have you been sick?"

She shrugged. "A couple days, *all* day. It's not fair."

"When is the last time you ate?"

"Is this twenty questions?"

"*When*, Tae?"

She rolled her eyes and sighed, then thought about it. The last thing she ate was cereal, and that had been… Wow, had it really been two days ago? "Tuesday."

"You haven't eaten, so you're weaker."

"I haven't been able to keep anything down, so I didn't bother."

"Don't you think you should talk to your doctor about this? It can't be healthy. You're eating for two." He picked up the washcloth and rang it out. She realized her blouse stood open, exposing her breasts. Good thing she'd wrestled a bra on that morning. When he leaned over and placed the cloth on her chest then reached behind her, a flick of his fingers relieved the clasp on her bra, and her nipples were in clear view for him.

She smacked his hands again and covered herself. "You just want to see me naked."

He grinned. "I'm not going to deny that, but I do want to help you, and I'm not going anywhere until you let me get you cleaned up and in fresh clothes. Then you're going to try some soup."

"I don't have the flu," she growled. Mustering the energy to drive him away or to get up did not work. She lay at his mercy. "You're the worst nurse."

He gave a bow of his head. "Thank you."

Tae didn't see how she could win the battle, so she gave into him. Jax removed her clothing from the waist up and took his time running the warm, soapy washcloth over her skin. She had to admit it felt good, and if she were not so ill, she might have liked his touch too. To her surprise, he didn't try anything funny, but she did notice his gaze lingering on her nipples, which made the traitorous buds tighten. Their doing so drew more of his attention, and the cycle continued.

At last, Jax brought a T-shirt from the bedroom and pulled it over her head. He removed her jeans but didn't replace them. When he reached for her panties, she drew the line. "No, absolutely not!"

He gave in. "Fine. Let me empty this, and I'll help you brush your teeth."

Tae imagined her light brown skin flamed red as he went through the steps of caring for her. His touch, rough as it was, seemed to settle her stomach, and soon he brought in a small bowl of soup and set it on the coffee table.

"Do you need me to feed you?"

"No. I can do it. I'm feeling a lot better." She was, and a "thank you" trembled on her tongue. Mumbling the words made him chuckle, and he cleaned up the tools of his nursing while she ate the soup with a spoon. Chicken and noodles never tasted so good, but she wondered if Jax could cook anything not from a can. She doubted it.

The evening passed with Jax staying and watching TV with her. Every time she looked at him, she willed herself to tell him the truth, that the baby was his, but her lips wouldn't part. Why was he there anyway? Did Daniel spill her secret, and Jax waited for her to admit it for herself? No, she believed Daniel when he said he wouldn't do that.

"Why are you here, Jax? Aren't you bored? I would think a man like you would be either starting his weekend early or planning it, trying to decide which woman to call."

He eyed her with a straight expression, one that revealed little of whether she had offended him. "Is that how you see me?"

"Isn't that you?"

"It is, normally."

"Nothing's changed."

"You're having a baby." He glanced at the TV screen. A commercial played for disposable diapers, of all things. Jax ran his palms over his thighs as if they were clammy. "I could be his or her daddy."

She blinked. He'd figured it out! This was the perfect time to come clean. She opened her mouth to speak, but he cut her off.

"I know I'm not, and I don't want to horn in on Daniel's territory, but well, I don't know how much he will be here for you and the baby with Alise to deal with."

Tae bit her lip. Jax still thought she'd slept with his best friend after he'd married Alise. What kind of women did he take her for? Or did he think she loved Daniel so much, marriage papers would mean nothing to her? She considered whether Jax thought he somehow protected his friend from the Jezebel by being at her place now. Thinking that way hurt her more after all he had done tonight than him calling her names. She wanted to tell him to leave, but again, since she was keeping the baby, he had a right to know she took care of herself on behalf of his child.

Her stomach growled, and she pressed a hand to it, embarrassed. "Wow, sickness gone, and I'm starving. Are you hungry? You've been here like three hours."

She stood up, and he reached out as if to steady her, but she was fine. He followed her to the kitchen, and she opened the freezer door. The compartment was filled with frozen dinners and a few meats she usually popped into the Crock-Pot on the rare occasions she felt like a more elaborate dinner with veggies. Cooking wasn't her forte.

"None of that looks healthy," he said, standing behind her.

A shiver tingled in her back at his nearness. "I never claimed to eat healthy. This body takes work to stay this way."

Jax's gaze raked her and paused at her ass. "Indeed."

"Stop staring."

He looked into her eyes. "Why should I?"

"I thought you were here to help me."

He walked around her and bumped the freezer door closed,

taking her hand in his. "I am, and the first place we'll start is with food."

"I was trying to do that."

"No." He shook his head and raised her hand toward his mouth, flipped it palm up, and nipped the inside of her wrist. She gasped and tried to pull away. He held on. "You need to eat healthier. I'm not saying one hundred percent perfect, but definitely not all sugar cereal and microwave meals."

"What do you know about my cereal, Jaxon Hart?" She grumbled that everyone her knew her habit.

"Enough." He spun her toward the exit and smacked her ass. "Go get some pants and shoes on. We're going to the grocery store."

"I have plenty of food!"

"You can go, or I can dress you. Just as a warning, it would be my pleasure."

"Like that's news." She muttered all the way down the hall to the bedroom and searched out pants and shoes. Knowing Jax waited for her in the living room for some reason brought back memories of the time Daniel had sent her to get dressed. That time she'd stripped instead and ended up losing her virginity. Being pregnant, her innocence was long gone, but she would not strip down for Jax tonight—*well, not again anyway.*

The grocery store was just two miles from Tae's apartment, and Jax insisted on driving them there. She didn't argue. They walked in together and grabbed a cart. "I hear if you shop only from the outside aisles, you'll get the healthiest foods," he said.

Tae rolled her eyes at him. "I'm getting my staples, and they're not from the outside aisles."

"We'll compromise."

She followed behind him while he selected celery, potatoes, onions, fruits of several kinds, and more. "You know that's going to cost a fortune, right?"

He ignored her and had the nerve to knock on a melon.

Tae listened to one when he did. "Do you know what you're listening for?"

He grinned. "No."

"Do you know how to cook?"

"No, again."

"So, you plan on me wasting money or the food going bad?"

"I guarantee, we'll eat everything."

"Who is this *we*?"

They bickered good-naturedly all over the store until Tae came to the baby aisle. She paused by the assortment of canned formula and frowned, reading the labels. Jax joined her. Feeling the heat of his body next to her did things to her libido. At least it wasn't dead yet.

"Do we know which one we will buy, or are you breastfeeding?" he asked.

He used that "we" again, and she chewed the inside of her cheek. "Don't they eventually have to have formula either way?"

"No idea."

Movement to their left caught Tae's eye, and she glanced over to see a blonde pushing a cart with a toddler in it. The tight, white T-shirt showed off enormous boobs and flat abs that looked like they'd never carried an infant behind them. While Tae took in the miracle that was the woman's physique and thought of her own already imperfect body, the woman glanced up and offered a friendly smile—at Jax.

"Hello." The husky voice made Tae want to choke her.

"Hello," Jax echoed.

Tae moved between them and placed a hand square in the center of Jax's chest. "Come on, honey. I don't think we need any formula for the baby. You can help me breastfeed." She side-eyed the mommy skank to be sure she got her meaning, and was satisfied with the heightened color in the pretty face. Tae brushed past Jax heading in the opposite direction and almost stumbled when her belly came into contact with is hard-on. She waited until they cleared the aisle and entered another one to round on him.

"Did you want to go back? I mean I don't want to keep you from anything!"

He blinked at her, and she eyed the front of his pants. The unrepentant man rocked on his heels and grinned. "You did say I could suck your nipples. What other reaction did you expect?"

This time it was her turn to blink. "What are you…? Oh!" She smacked his arm. "I said the baby. Get your mind out the gutter."

He shrugged. "I don't remember you saying the baby at all."

She shook her head and started down the aisle. "You make no sense."

"Then what's that laugh for?"

"I am not amused," she insisted.

"Yes, my queen."

Tae stopped short, forgetting their conversation. "Wait, I think I need these."

He looked over her shoulder and then picked up the package. "Nursing pads?"

For some reason, she didn't feel embarrassed to talk to him about it. "Not now, but maybe in a few weeks. I'm not sure. Maybe I should get them now."

He picked up the box and dropped them in the cart. "Better safe than use a maxipad."

This time she did laugh out loud. "Only you would think of that, Jax."

"I'm not ashamed of it."

"I can see that."

"You seem to have a lot of bits and pieces of information but nothing solid. I thought you had two sisters with children."

She winced at his candor. "I do, but I didn't spend a lot of time with them when they were pregnant. By then, I was already in Charlotte, and they live back in New Jersey. We talk on the phone occasionally, and sometimes I visit at holidays, but that's all I can stand."

"Tae, don't you need them at a time like this?" She was surprised to hear sympathy in his tone, and possibly worry.

"You wouldn't understand." Her phone dinged and buzzed, and she pulled it from her purse to check the display. A text message had come in from Zerita an hour ago, which she hadn't heard, saying her friend would be flying back home tomorrow. The latest message came from Janita. She showed it to Jax. "Read this."

He read out loud. "Hey, sis. Can you send me a new iPhone or buy one online to deliver here to me? I dropped mine in the street and didn't have insurance. The iPhone 5c is great."

Jax looked at her like he couldn't believe what he had just read. Tae nabbed her phone from his hand and proceeded to delete the message. "That's why I don't speak to her often. No, hey, how are you doing? Are you dead or alive? Just buy me a six hundred dollar phone because you got it like that."

Jax rubbed his neck. "Doesn't she have a husband?"

"Yup." Tae headed toward the cereal aisle. Jax redirected her away from Frosted Flakes when she got there. "She does have a husband, but he doesn't make a lot of money. Last I heard she thought he had a mistress, as if a man at the lower part of middle class could have a 'mistress.'" She stabbed the air making quotes, her anger rising.

The next words she intended to utter were swept away when he drew her into his arms and kissed her lips. Tae pushed at Jax's chest and freed her mouth. She panted, trying to calm her racing pulse. "We're in public."

His voice dropped low and deep. "Want to continue it in private?"

"No." She pulled free of his hold, and he let her go without a struggle. "We can't continue where we left off at the hotel, Jax."

"Why? Because you want to save yourself for Daniel?"

She pressed her lips together and turned away from him. Snatching a box of her favorite snack from the shelf, she shoved the cart. Jax caught her hand and pulled her to a stop.

"I'm sorry. That was uncalled for."

She looked away from his eyes. "Maybe you should drop me home and forget this plan."

"Let me make it up to you. You're still hungry, and you have to eat. *Real food.*"

"Jax."

"Tae, I'm going to be around. The sooner you accept it, the better. I don't have to share your bed. I would never force my way there unless you invited me, but I'm going to support you, as a friend."

She glanced at him. Was he saying he wanted to sleep with her again? Sure there were sparks between them, but they had complicated their lives enough with sex. No, she would not give in to physical needs again, definitely not with Jax.

"You still don't know how to cook."

He took control of the cart and kissed her cheek. The sensations that arrowed through her system were no less intense than when their lips locked. "We'll bumble through together."

Chapter Ten

"Octavia, what are you doing carrying those bags?"

"Tae, let me get those for you."

Tae stopped dead in her tracks outside her apartment building. She looked first right to see Daniel heading toward her and then left to find Jax. What the hell were they both doing here? Did they plan it? She licked her lips and shifted the bags she held from one hand to the other but made no more moves as they approached. The answer to her questions were soon provided when Jax glared at Daniel over Tae's head.

"Why are you here?" Jax snapped. "Don't you have a wife?"

Daniel reddened. "I could ask the same of you."

"I don't have a wife."

"No, but what happened between you and Tae was a mistake, a moment of weakness that won't be repeated."

Jax's eyes narrowed. "Is that what she told you?"

"Boys, for real?" Tae interjected. "I know you two aren't going to argue outside my apartment."

Daniel didn't spare her a glance but stepped around her to get into Jax's face. He used two fingers to poke Jax's chest. Even she knew that was just asking for trouble. "You don't have any shame about it. You never apologized."

Jax laughed, a cold sound without humor. "Apologize to who? You? I notice you're not concerned about your vows but you want to claim I'm wrong. That's hilarious. And you have two seconds to back off before I make you sorry you showed up here today."

"I won't be the one who's sorry," Daniel shot back.

Tae grabbed Daniel's arm and pulled. "Stop! You two are like brothers. You can't fight."

Daniel made a rude noise. "Brothers? A brother wouldn't fuck your girl."

"Newsflash, asshole," Jax growled. "She's not your girl."

"If I have anything to say about it, she'll never be yours." Daniel followed his declaration with his fist, connecting with Jax's chin. Tae screamed at the sound of the impact, but as hard as it seemed, Jax only staggered back. He didn't miss a beat when he lunged and landed a blow into Daniel's side. Daniel crumpled but recovered fast. Both men's hands came up, fists clenched, mouths tight and eyes narrowed. They lowered their chins and tucked their elbows in close to their sides. They looked like prizefighters in dress clothes, and Tae had to put a stop to it.

She dropped her bags on the ground and stepped in between the two of them. Jax's fist just missed her head, and she squeaked. Both men dropped back, but Jax was the first to dart forward and draw her into his arms. "Tae, are you crazy? I could have hit you!" He studied her face and head as if the wind flying off his fist could have damaged her somehow. She glared up at him.

"If you weren't fighting, I wouldn't be at risk. Now stop this. Both of you." She peered from one to the other, and neither said a word. Tae pulled herself from Jax's hold. "Fine, then you can both be fools alone. I'm going in the house."

She bent to get her bags, and both men tried to take them from her. She smacked their hands, gathered her stuff, and charged into the building without a backward glance. When she made it up to the second floor where she lived, she stretched to look out the gigantic window above the stairs, which overlooked the parking lot. Jax and Daniel stood there glaring lasers at each other. Then Daniel said something, and Jax replied. A moment of tension made her think they would go at it again, but then the two men spun away from each other to return to their cars. Tae breathed a sigh of relief and let herself into her apartment. How had it come down to this? She had never respected women who let men fight over her, and here she was in the middle feeling stuck and unable to get out of the situation.

Tae refused calls from both Daniel and Jax the rest of the evening, and the next morning, she went into work and plopped down in Zerita's office, kicked off her shoes, and drew her feet up.

"Make yourself comfortable," Zerita teased.

"I will." Tae snagged a piece of chocolate from the dish next to her and unraveled the wrapper to pop the treat into her mouth. She let the candy sit on her tongue melting and soothing her mood. "I'm so glad you have an office. One day I will be promoted to senior editor, and I'll have a private office." While she'd gotten the position of editor, it did not come with an office at her magazine, but Tae had known that beforehand. She might have a lowly cubicle, but she still loved her job.

Zerita smiled. "Definitely. So, about the baby?"

"How was your trip? Meet any cute guys from other mags?"

Her friend turned from studying the computer screen and folded her hands on the desk. "Tae."

"I know, I know." Tae sat up and put her feet on the floor. The love seat sat across from Zerita's desk, and the office was still big enough to have floor space and visitor chairs this side of the desk. The walls were lined with bookshelves, all crammed full of books, magazines, and manuals. On top of that, there was an incredible view of uptown Charlotte from the window. Tae enjoyed relaxing in Zerita's office, and her friend had told her she was welcome at any time to unwind, but right now, Tae couldn't get rid of the tension between her shoulders.

"Tae, are you keeping the baby?"

"Yes."

"And?"

"Why does there have to be an and?"

"Girl, I know you, and I can feel it. There's more."

"Okay, Miss Cleo."

Zerita pursed her lips. Tae gave in and told her about Daniel and Jax, their interest in her and how they'd fallen into a physical fight over her the night before.

"And how did that make you feel?"

"Are you my therapist now?"

"Don't make me come over this desk."

Tae laughed. "Frustrated, angry…"

"Flattered."

Tae stiffened. "I'm not pitting them against each other if that's what you're getting at."

"Octavia Croft, lie to yourself, but don't lie to me."

"I'm not lying to you or myself. I didn't ask for this."

"But you're not ending it either."

"How can I? Neither one of them will listen to me."

Zerita scraped her chair back and stood. Her pinched mouth and eyes shooting sparks meant she was pissed at Tae. She turned toward the window as if looking at Tae would make *her* ready to fight. "You say you're not playing Daniel and Jax off each other, but you still haven't told Jax he's your baby's daddy. Why not?"

"I—"

"What kind of signal do you think you're giving Daniel by not telling Jax the truth? That you want him to be the daddy. Or did you sleep with him and don't want to admit it?"

Tae surged to her feet. "Of course not! I thought you of all people would—"

"Come off the high horse, Tae. I believe you. That doesn't change the fact, from what you've told me, you let him come around and play daddy. You're going to tell me he doesn't have expectations after that?"

Tae didn't try to respond. She knew Zerita was right. Leave it to her friend not to bite her tongue and to lay everything out the way it was. Why hadn't she told Jax? Because it would mean he'd know his rights and stick around? Was she hoping for Daniel to be the daddy no matter what? She thought about her time with Jax and their grocery shopping. They had both been so ignorant but willing to learn. She admitted they had a lot of fun together, the way they had in the past, laughing together, taking nothing seriously. Her relationship with Daniel was different. Daniel cared for her like a delicate flower, and she loved him so much. What he had wanted in the past was happening now, although she hadn't planned it.

"Maybe you're right. Maybe I do want what I threw away. I know you're going to say what about Alise, and I'm trying to think about her, but I can't. I hated her from the start."

"If you liked her, would it have made a difference?"

"I don't know."

Zerita appeared calmer. She sat down again and faced Tae. "Let's look at it logically. If you tell Jax the truth, will things change between you?"

"He might hate me for keeping it from him for so long."

"So?"

Tae blinked at her.

Zerita sighed. "You like the attention. You want both of them to want you. The fact is you never would have slept with Jax if you didn't feel something for him. You're not the type of woman who sleeps around and definitely not without some type of emotional tie. It's not just physical pleasure with you."

Zerita knew her too damn well. Sometimes she wondered if her friend knew her better than she knew herself. "I don't have feelings for Jax. I like him. He's a lot of fun, and I see him trying. It's sweet."

Zerita eyed her.

"Fine. I'm attracted to him. That's it. I'm not getting off on them both paying me attention. I don't care what you say. It killed me to see them fighting. They're like brothers, and I don't want to ruin it."

"You should have considered that when you broke the unwritten code." Zerita turned to her computer screen, and her fingers flew over the keys. "Tell him, Tae. He deserves it. If you end up with Daniel, that's on the two of you, but you can't block Jax from knowing about his baby. It's not right, and you'll never fully live with yourself if you don't. Now get out of my office. If you need further counseling, the doctor is in after six, at home, and she accepts bottles of wine as payment."

Tae harrumphed. "I think the doctor needs to have her license revoked for extortion."

Zerita saluted, and Tae slipped her feet into her shoes and left the office. She returned to her cubicle in time to see her cell phone ringing. Speak of the devil, Jax's name flashed on the screen. She slid her finger across the phone toward the X and set the phone aside. Then she brought up the document she'd been working on the day before. The article on preparing to see your ex was so interesting and entertaining, she'd had to read it several times just to edit rather than get lost in the advice and equate the examples to her own experience. When the phone beeped, she found Jax had left a message. Time to face the music.

❧

"Mm," Tae moaned around a mouthful of beef curry. "This is so good."

Jax stared at her lips as she chewed. "I like the way you enjoy your food."

"Dirty mind." She laughed.

He shrugged. "I make no excuses. After all I brought you here because you wanted a break from the food we make together at home."

Her heart beat faster at the way he said it, as if they lived together. They didn't, but he was at her apartment often enough, and they had looked up a ton of recipes online and learned to prepare them side by side. She had to give it to him. Jax made eating healthier more fun, and she hadn't gained too much weight even though she was now four months pregnant. The changes in her body surprised her in the way she responded to them. She'd thought she would hate her belly growing and her breasts getting heavier. She didn't. Jax and Daniel both had said she looked even more beautiful and that her skin glowed. Still, her reason for liking her body had nothing to do with what they thought.

Tonight, she had brought Jax out to ONE-U, the Japanese restaurant she loved, in order to come clean. She had put it off for weeks after discussing the topic countless times with Zerita. No more. Tonight was the night.

Thinking about her resolution produced butterflies in her belly, and she placed her chopsticks on the side of the plate. Jax paused in the act of eating his udon. "What's wrong? Portion too big?"

She examined the massive plate, filled with beef, rice, potatoes, onions, and other veggies. "It's big, and I usually take some home, but I eat more than this."

"What's up?" He reached across the table and touched her hand. A tremor passed through her fingers, and he gripped them in a strong hold. She dropped her gaze to her lap and saw the slight swelling to her belly. The base was now firm, and her ankles were sometimes swollen but not all the time. She took in a deep breath and looked up at him. As soon as she opened her mouth, he spoke again. "I know what will make you feel better."

Her eyes widened. "What?"

He bent toward the floor and brought up the paper bag he'd carried into the restaurant with them. Tae hadn't known what to think of the package but was so nervous about her intention to tell him about the baby, she didn't question him. Now he unraveled the brown paper bag and reached inside. He wiggled his eyebrows and grinned at her, making a big production about it. The next thing she knew he withdrew a colorful baby toy. Tae burst out laughing.

"It's…" she began. "What is it?"

He pointed out the features of the caterpillar handle with various colored rings around its body and the musical notes on the front of the toy. "See? It's like a radio. There's an on and off switch and a volume control. It plays seven different tunes to drive you crazy when the baby plays them over and over."

Tae shook her head. "Aw, that's so sweet. I can't believe you bought that. The baby will love it, and you're probably right. After a while I'll want to toss it out the window."

Jax glared at her and held the toy protectively against his chest. "But you won't, right, Mommy?"

Something tightened in her chest. *No, Daddy*. "I won't."

His cell phone rang. He held up a finger. "One second while I get rid of this call."

Tae almost fell over on the table, but she welcomed the interruption. Why was this a big deal? Maybe because she'd put it off and she feared Jax's anger. They got along so well when he wasn't arguing with Daniel about seeing her.

"Jax here. Yeah, Frank, what's up?" Jax paused, listening into his phone. He looked across at Tae and winked at her. Once again, her heart stirred, and she lowered her gaze to her plate. Jax continued talking, and she didn't pay much attention until the tone of his voice changed. "Damn, you're right. I can't miss this opportunity. I'm on it."

He disconnected the call, and Tae sensed their night out had come to an end, but what surprised her was how disappointed she felt. "You have to go?"

He nodded. "I'm so sorry. I wouldn't go if I hadn't been trying to catch up with this guy for a couple months. He knows someone has been on his trail—me. My friend just informed me of where he's holed up, and I need to get there before he moves again."

"No problem. I understand." She signaled for the waitress.

"I'll drop you home first," he offered as he pulled his wallet from his back pocket. "Tae, can I come by later tonight?"

She hesitated, but she needed to talk to him. "Yes, you can come. Don't be too late."

"I promise. I won't be."

By midnight, Jax hadn't shown up, and Tae refused to call him. She went to bed cursing his name.

Chapter Eleven

"Tae, are you there?"

She moaned and cracked an eye open to check the time. Six a.m., way too early for Daniel to be calling her. Yawning, she considered sitting up and dismissed the idea. In a minute she'd tell him where to go and throw her cell phone across the room before going back to sleep.

"You must be out of your mind calling me so early, Daniel Elliott."

"Tae, Jax has been shot."

Her stomach knotted so tight, she almost threw up. All sense of sleepiness left in an instant, and she jumped to her feet. The room swirled and then righted itself. This time her stomach somersaults were the result of morning sickness, but it quickly subsided, thank goodness. "Is he okay? What happened? Daniel, tell me he's fine!"

Daniel was silent a heartbeat, and she feared the worst. "He's okay. I'm on my way to pick you up."

"I can drive myself. Which hospital?"

"Huntersville."

"I'll be there." She disconnected the line and shot to the bathroom. Prayers that Jax would be okay ran through her mind over and over. She hadn't told him she was having his baby. What if he died without knowing? No, she had to believe he would be all right. If it were critical, surely Daniel would have told her. Or maybe he didn't want to scare her without being there in person. *Don't think that way, Tae. He's got to be fine. Think positive.*

She dressed in record time and stuffed her feet into slippers when she couldn't find her other sandal. Keys in hand and purse swinging behind her as she ran, she left the apartment. East Charlotte to Huntersville was a good twenty-five minutes with moderate traffic. At just after six in the morning, she had open roads, and she took advantage of them with her foot heavy on the accelerator. All the way, she prayed and begged for Jax. When she hurtled through the emergency-room doors, her throat dry and chest heaving, she scanned the waiting area for Daniel.

He stood just outside the doors leading past triage and frowned at her when she ran up to him. "Calm down, Tae. Why are you dressed like that?"

She ignored his question. "I want to see him."

Once again, Daniel seemed put out with her concern, but he nodded and glanced at the nurse who buzzed them to the back. Tae clung to Daniel's arm, feeling unsteady and sick. Her belly ached, and it seemed like all the energy had been drained out of her. Pregnancy meant constant exhaustion, and losing sleep, even an hour, made it much worse. Right now, she didn't matter. Jax did. If he were on the brink of death, by now surely Daniel would admit it before she went to see him, but he was unusually quiet. Maybe Jax being shot affected him more than it did her. *Of course it did. They've been friends for years.*

Daniel thrust aside a curtain leading into one of the examining rooms, but the bed lay empty. He whirled to face the nurse's station, his face a thundercloud, but a perky little nurse headed him off. "Oh, Daniel, your friend has been moved into a room on the second floor. If you'll hold on a minute, I'll get the exact number."

Tae stared after her as she headed to the station. "Daniel?" she said, pursing her lips.

He rubbed the back of his neck and shrugged. "I guess I was a little chatty when I was worried about that idiot."

"Just how long did you wait to call me?"

His eyes were apologetic. "Not long. An artery was nicked, and there was a lot of blood…"

Tae had already been feeling a bit queasy with the hospital smell of disinfectant and latex. Daniel's talk of blood did not help. "I got it. Let's go."

They reached Jax's room at last, and seeing that it wasn't located in the ICU gave her some relief. Jax lay in the bed with his eyes closed and his hands resting on his lap. A bandage stretched across his shoulder and down his right arm. His skin, usually tanned, glimmered pale under the LED lights.

Tae sat gingerly on the side of the bed and took Jax's hand in hers. "What happened?" she whispered.

Jax's eyes opened and captured her. He stared at her, and she looked back, silent and overcome with myriad emotions. After a few moments of him holding her prisoner, he released her and let his gaze lower to her chest. "Your shirt is on the wrong side."

Tae looked down and frowned. He was right. That's why Daniel had asked why she was dressed that way. "I'm not here for a beauty pageant. I'm here to see why you would go and get yourself shot! How are you? What happened?"

Jax smiled and shifted his position a little. His wince of pain made her do the same and squeeze his fingers. He rubbed her hand with his thumb as if to comfort her. "The guy I was looking for didn't want to be found."

Tae trembled.

"Shh, it's fine. I got him before he got me."

"He did get you," she blurted.

"Only my shoulder. I'll be good as new before you know it."

She tugged her hand free of his and turned away. "Stop being flip, Jax. You're not invincible. This proves it, and your job is too dangerous. I don't know what I would have done if you…"

Daniel made a noise nearby. Tae looked up in time to see him disappearing through the doorway. "Going to find…" he said, pulling the door closed. She didn't catch the last part he'd said. Jax touched her clenched fingers on her lap.

"Tae, look at me."

A tear slid down her cheek. She sniffed and wiped it away. "You keep trying to be there for me, but how will you do that if you're gone?" She couldn't bring herself to say dead. Just the thought was too much, and realizing she cared about him threw her for a loop. She couldn't call it love exactly, but Jax was a good man. He was special and important to her, more so to his son or daughter.

"I said look at me." The stern tone brought her chin up, but she met his slight smile. "I'm not going anywhere. I promise."

"You didn't keep your promise last night."

"Ouch, you're harder on me than the bullet."

"So not funny."

"Sorry." He touched her cheek. "Are you going to forgive me, or do I have to use my charms?"

She rolled her eyes, looking him up and down, dressed in the hospital gown. "You think you can pull off a statement like that dressed the way you are? That gown won't get you on the cover of *GQ* magazine."

"The nurses aren't complaining."

She stood up.

"Tae, marry me."

Her mouth fell open, but she lost the ability to move.

"Give me a chance. I know I can make you happy, and I'll be there to take care of you."

She rounded on him. "I don't need to be taken care of, Jax. I'm a grown woman. Besides, you're only here because I'm pregnant."

"Is that so wrong?"

"No."

"The baby will have an easier time if he or she has both a mom and dad present."

She didn't want or expect declarations of love from Jax, but damn, couldn't he have pretended for a moment? Despite what she'd said about the hospital gown, he was sexy as hell. She just bet the nurses were falling all over themselves for him, just as that one nurse had done with Daniel downstairs. Jax would eat it up and flirt without reservation. Daniel hadn't exactly denied flirting while he waited to know his friend was okay. "I'm not marrying anyone for that reason."

To her surprise, Jax frowned. "If Daniel asked you, you would say yes."

"Excuse me?" She put her hands on her hips. "Maybe you forgot he asked me three years ago, and I turned him down then."

"Things change." He glanced at her swollen belly, and her heart sank. "Daniel still loves you. He's proven that chasing after you. Maybe it's time you give in."

"I'll thank you not to make decisions for my life. Feel better."

She left the room and kept walking until she reached her car outside and drove back home. Let them comfort each other. She needed a break and sleep. When she'd called in to work to tell her boss she had a family emergency and should be in by ten, then was lying in bed drifting off to sleep, did the full impact of Jax's proposal hit her. He had asked her to marry him, and she'd blown it off like she received offers every day of the week!

❖

"Crud, I forgot the dressing," Tae said as she set the huge bowl of tossed salad on the dining room table next to the platter of pulled beef.

Daniel pushed his chair back and stood. "I'll get it."

Jax made a gagging noise, and Daniel glared at him. Jax raised his eyebrows. "Is there a problem?"

"Yeah, you," Daniel snapped. "Why are you here?"

Jax surged to his feet. "Why are *you* here? Don't you have a wife?"

Daniel didn't even redden this time around. Tae guessed he was done being shamed. "The only reason you're hanging around her is because you've always wanted what's mine."

"When the fuck did she become yours?" Jax growled back.

"Boys!" Tae had gone to get the dressing herself and slammed it down on the table. "Both of you are going to be outside hungry in a minute. Try me."

They lowered their gazes to the table in unison and muttered their apologies. Tae stroked her belly. She hadn't meant for this to happen, her seeing both of them almost nightly, both running errands for her, shopping with her. Jax even rubbed her feet, but neither of the men were willing to give an inch. At least they hadn't come to blows again, but she had to break up arguments too often.

Jax pulled out a chair for her. "Here. Sit down. Let me finish whatever else you need done."

She took him up on the offer of a seat. Her feet ached. "I'm done. We have everything we need. I just don't want you two fighting anymore tonight." Tears filled her eyes, and she blinked them away, annoyed. They appeared too often lately. "Can you do that for me?"

"Of course, baby," Jax said. Before she realized what he would do, he kissed her lips. He drew back, a look of surprise on his face and glanced at Daniel. She did as well, but her ex-boyfriend's face held no expression.

"No more fighting tonight," Daniel said.

Tae rubbed a twinge in her side and then began serving the three of them. Daniel reached across the table and relieved her of the serving spoon. While he piled their plates with food, Jax poured himself and Daniel a glass of wine and her a glass of grape juice. She raised her glass to take a sip, watching them over the rim. Things had begun to change. She still loved Daniel without a doubt, but as she turned her gaze to Jax, she couldn't deny wanting to keep him a part of her life. What did it mean? Was it just because of their connection with the baby?

She dismissed thoughts of the two men and tucked into her food. When they were done, Daniel sent her to the living room to relax, and the two men cleared the table and stacked dishes into the dishwasher. Tae strained her ears to catch whether they fought in the kitchen, but she couldn't hear anything. A short while later, Jax walked into the living room and sat at the foot of the couch and pulled her feet into his lap. He removed her thick socks from her feet since she tended to walk around the apartment in them rather than shoes. Daniel joined them sitting at the head of the couch, and he drew her head onto his lap. Jax glared at him, but he didn't say anything.

"Mm, that feels good," she murmured as Jax began massaging her feet. Both men shifted on the chair, and Tae's heel brushed something hard. She raised an eyebrow at Jax, and he winked, not sorry in the least. Deciding to ignore his physical response to her moan, she turned her attention to the TV and flipped channels, but nothing distracted her from the tingles Jax's strong hands sent to her nether regions.

When she landed on the health channel, she was reminded of Jax's injury. He was mostly better now with time passed, but sometimes she saw how stiff his shoulder seemed. She drew her feet away from him. "That's enough."

He looked up. "Did I hurt you?"

"No." She sat up, and both men moved closer to her while she sat in the middle of the couch. Sighing, she shook her head. Jax took her hand in his and held it. With Jax around, Daniel never tried to touch her intimately, but she often felt his gaze on her, and she'd noticed as much as with Jax the tent in his pants. The worse part of all of this was her own horniness. Being pregnant seemed to have made her desires skyrocket, but so far she hadn't given into either man. She used her own fingers to get herself off. That did not do much when two hard, male thighs bumped hers on both sides. Longing made her panties damp. Jax escalated the problem by caressing the inside of her wrist with his thumb. The bastard played dirty.

Tae drew her feet beneath her and rubbed her belly. She yawned, her eyelids drooping. Next week, she would be twenty weeks, and she had a doctor appointment to see what the sex of her baby was. She bit her lip.

"My appointment next week…"

"I'm going."

"I'm going."

She tensed. Both men had spoken at the same time. She groaned and rubbed her forehead. Somehow up until now she'd avoided having them both at the appointments at the same time. Jax attended more often than not because his schedule was flexible, and Daniel hadn't pushed.

Jax laid a hand on her thigh, and Daniel laid his on her other thigh. She shut her eyes. If she came right now, it was both their faults. A cramp in her side made her forget about sex, and she winced, rubbing it.

"What's wrong, Tae?" Jax sat forward and pressed a hand over hers.

"Nothing. I'm fine. Just a little crampy."

"You should go to bed," Daniel suggested. "*Alone.*"

"Don't start!" She moaned when the pain intensified.

Jax jumped from the couch and whipped her into his arms. He charged down the hall toward her bedroom and kicked the half-open door inward. Tae found herself dumped on the bed, not roughly but not gentle either. The knitted brows over Jax's eyes told her he was worried. He walked over to the dresser as Daniel entered the room and rummaged through her drawers. When he pulled out a nightgown, Tae opened her mouth to protest. Jax had her blouse off in seconds, cutting across her protest.

"Get her some fresh socks," Jax ordered.

Daniel moved to do as he asked without complaining. With Daniel bent over his task at the dresser, Jax pulled the nightgown over her head, and with deft fingers reached beneath it to unhook her bra. He tucked her between the sheets, and she squeaked, eyes widening when he nabbed her panties and slid them down her legs. By the time Daniel turned around frowning at them with socks in hand, Jax had her panties balled up in his palm.

"Maybe you need to go to the doctor," Daniel said.

Tae clutched the sheet to her chin and lay on her pillows. "I just need rest."

Both men stood over her bed watching her. She squirmed, feeling exposed.

"You can go. I'm all right." The pains had eased, but her body was on fire for a whole other reason than her health. "T-Thanks for taking care of me."

Daniel nodded. He flipped the bottom of the sheet up and slipped her socks onto her feet while Jax watched as if he were judging whether Daniel did it right. *Or making sure Daniel doesn't feel me up.* Remembering the way Jax had removed her underwear had her squeezing her legs together. They needed to go.

"Good night."

Jax chuckled. "Fine. I can take a hint. Come on, Daniel."

Daniel glared at him, but he started for the door with Jax following.

"Jax," she called.

He stopped and looked back at her.

"My hamper is over there in the closet, perv."

Amusement lit his green eyes. "Oh, you don't want me to leave your clothes on the floor. Got it." He knew what she meant. She watched to make sure he dropped the panties he still held in his hand, along with her T-shirt, bra, and pants into the basket. Then he leaned over her and planted a soft kiss to her lips before leaving. "Good night, beautiful. I'll call you tomorrow."

Her breath hitched in her chest, and she nodded. They left, and she lay in bed lonelier than she ever remembered feeling in her life. She turned onto her side and let her body sink into the groove she'd made in the mattress. She missed lying on her stomach and hated the aches and pains that came with shifting of her hip bones to make room for the baby. When sleep didn't come quickly as it usually did, she reached for her cell phone and sifted through the favorites list. Her mom picked up on the third ring.

"I can't believe it. Is this my daughter Octavia calling me?"

"Dramatic much, Ma?" Tae smiled. "How are you and Dad?"

"We're alive. Not in the grave yet."

Tae rolled her eyes.

"Your sister called me and said she asked you for help, but you ignored her. I worry about Janita." Tae heard the concern in her mother's voice.

"But you don't worry about me. She has a husband, Ma, and I'm not paying for a new phone for her."

"I do worry about you, Tae, but you've always been strong. I know you are doing well for yourself."

"Apparently, everybody thinks I'm well, asking me to shell out six hundred dollars."

"Terrence is only working part-time. They have to take care of themselves and the babies."

"You mean the teenagers."

"Tae."

"What?" Tae sighed and rubbed her belly. Why did she call now? She should have just waited until her mind settled down and she fell asleep. "I don't want to argue about Janita. She can take care of herself, and if she would get a job, she wouldn't be looking to everybody else in the family for money all the time. I'm sorry. I gave her all I'm giving. I've cut her off."

"Well, you have to do what you think is best, sweetie."

Tae thought her mother didn't agree with her choice. Well they could all get over it. She needed to save for her own baby. Janita's oldest was sixteen for goodness sake. She could get a job herself.

"Ma, I wanted to ask you something."

"What's that, sweetie?"

She hesitated and then plunged ahead. "This is going to sound crazy at my age, but... Ugh. Okay, how do I know when I'm really in love with the right one? I mean, you and Dad have been together since the beginning of time and..."

"Thanks, sweetheart."

Tae chuckled at her mother's dry tone.

"Are you in love, Tae? I remember how hurt you were when you broke up with Daniel. I liked him. I thought he was a wonderful man, and even Dad said you let a good one go. He could have been the one."

"Okay, Ma, I get it."

"He got married though, so he's off the market."

Tae wondered where her mother had heard that news. She never told her. "How do you know?"

"Oh we talk sometimes."

Tae's throat closed. She swallowed. "Excuse me?"

"I called him not long ago to see how he was doing. We had a nice long talk. He told me he married. I congratulated him. To be honest, he didn't seem all that happy, but I encouraged him to keep working at it. Marriage is no picnic. I can tell you."

If Tae didn't cut her off, she'd keep rambling on. "What else did he tell you?"

"What else was there for him to tell me?"

Damn, her mother was clever when she wanted to be. "I just wanted to know about love."

"I think you know what love is. You loved him, Tae. You may still love him. Is there someone else?"

With every passing moment, she regretted asking the question.

"You never talk to me," her mother complained. "I used to always hear your news from Janita or your younger sister, Sasha." *As if I don't know who Sasha is without her explaining.*

"I'm sorry, Ma."

"You were a closed-off little girl coming up, always wanting your own space. You would hide in the closet to get it, but Janita and Sasha would find you and pick at you until you gave in and joined the family. I put it down to being a middle child."

Tae rolled to her back and stared at the ceiling, letting her mother ramble on. Her personality was what it was and wouldn't change this late in the game. She loved her family, but her mother was right, she'd fought for her own and lost the battle too many times. She hadn't told her mother about the baby, and now didn't seem like a good time. Her mother would be thrilled, but she would no doubt descend upon Tae with others in tow. Tae wasn't ready for that, not with her emotional tug-o-war over Jax and Daniel.

Her mother broke through her wandering thoughts, and Tae realized she'd started to drift off. "You will know when you love *the one*, Tae. Just trust your heart. It will never lead you wrong."

"Thanks, Ma. Well, I'll talk to you later. I'm going to get some sleep because I have to be in early tomorrow."

"Okay, sweetie. Call more often. I love you."

"I love you, too. Good night."

"'Night."

Tae disconnected the call and dropped the phone at her side. Exhaustion hit her hard, and she decided she'd put the phone on the nightstand in a minute. She shut her eyes and fell into a deep sleep.

Chapter Twelve

The jagged pains across Tae's belly woke her from sleep. She cried out, fear gripping her chest. This should not be happening. What was this pain? Blowing out shallow breaths, she tried to roll over from her back, and another cramp dropped her flat again. She pushed a hand beneath her hip to give herself a bit of leverage, and her fingers touched something damp. She froze. *Can't be, can't be!*

Feeling something hard on her other side, she realized she'd fallen asleep with her phone in the bed. Somehow she worked it out from under her and dialed Jax. He answered on the first ring, his voice thick with sleep.

"Tae, baby, what is it?"

She burst into tears. "Jax, I think something's wrong. It hurts so bad, and I think… I don't know. Please come get me."

"I'm on my way. Don't move, baby. I have the key. I'll let myself in."

She had argued with him when he insisted on making a copy of her apartment key. Jax wouldn't let it go. He claimed she might need him unexpectedly, and she'd told him he just wanted to come and go as if he lived there. The man had had the nerve to tell her he didn't care what she thought of his motives. He wanted to be sure he could get to her if he needed to. Now she was glad she'd given in to his bullying.

Sobbing but trying her best to calm down, Tae waited what seemed like an eternity. She took Jax's advice not to move, hoping and praying it would save her baby's life. *Please, please…anything…I'll do anything.*

The front door banged against the wall, and she jumped. Seconds later, Jax rushed into the room and flipped the light on. He bent over her, touched her cheek, and whispered words of comfort she couldn't understand, but she saw his expression, the anguish and tears when he examined the bed.

"No, no, no," he whispered, this time his voice a concentration of pain. "We don't have time to get you dressed. I'm going to wrap you in a blanket."

He did, and soon they descended the stairs to the first floor and out to his car. Jax drove like a demon all the way to the hospital, running red lights. Tae shut her eyes, trying her best to hold onto the strap and her belly at the same time. As he drove, Jax's hand covered hers, and he never stopped talking to her. His smooth, deep voice kept her from panicking.

When they screeched into the hospital parking lot, Jax barely made time to park before he ran around to her side of the car and scooped her into his arms. She marveled at the care he took not to jostle her when his usual way was so rough.

He barreled through the emergency room entrance, demanding service. "She's cramping and bleeding. I need someone to look at her, now!" Nurses scrambled. Soon Tae found herself ensconced in a bed and a doctor examining her.

After a tense few moments when he asked her questions, the man looked up. Tae crushed Jax's hand in her hold, but he never even winced. She shook from head to toe and pulled Jax's hand to her cheek, desperate to absorb some of his strength.

"Your baby's heartbeat is steady, and there's been no major change in the condition of the amniotic sac. However, there has been as you've noted some leakage. I'm prescribing rest and absolutely no stress. You must remain calm. This is important for the health of your baby. Do you understand?"

Tae resented the condescending attitude, but she nodded her head. "For the rest of the term?"

"Not necessarily. Your regular doctor can monitor you, but for now you need to take a few days to put your feet up and stay in bed."

"She will get the rest," Jax promised.

"Good." The doctor scribbled something on his clipboard. "It's a good idea to see your regular doctor, no longer than a day or two from now."

"Of course." Tae sighed and lay back on her pillow. She loosened the death grip she had on Jax's hand, and he flexed his fingers. "Sorry."

He grinned and brushed the sweaty hair off her forehead. "Don't worry about it. I didn't feel a thing."

"Because you're Superman?"

He stroked her cheek and then touched her belly. "Because I was terrified. I'm a man, but I'm only human."

Her heart stirred. She recalled how he looked like he would cry. Jax thought the baby was Daniel's, but he loved the little one, maybe as much as she did.

He lifted her hand to his mouth and kissed it. "I'm going to go out and call Daniel. He should know."

"Wait."

He had started for the door but stopped and turned back. "What is it? Do I need to call the doctor back in?"

"No, not that." A cramp rolled through her belly, and she breathed deep, shutting her eyes.

"Tae, whatever you're stressing about, stop it. You heard the doctor. I'm going to be right there to make sure you do as he says."

She opened here eyes, looking at him. "I'm not going to fight it. Trust me. This scared the crap out of me, and I don't want to do anything to jeopardize m-my…" She hesitated.

"Tae?" He leaned close. "Baby, what's wrong."

"It's your baby, Jax," she blurted out. "You're the father. I never slept with Daniel—I mean not after we broke up."

The silence was deafening.

He straightened and moved away from the bed, stuffed his hands in his pockets, and said nothing. She could no longer see his face and worried about his reaction. What was he thinking? Did he hate her? Of course he did. For almost five months she'd let him believe the baby he loved wasn't his but his best friend's. In fairness, she hadn't known until she was two months pregnant, but three months was too long.

"I'm so sorry. I was wrong to keep it from you. I have no excuse."

"You're right. You don't," he interjected, and she felt tears start that she blinked away. He heaved his shoulders and rolled his neck, then turned back to her. The smile on his lips didn't reflect in his eyes. They appeared sad, but the sadness vanished, hidden away she knew because he wanted her to stop worrying. "We're going to concentrate on you and the baby."

She couldn't help it. She cried, and he sank onto the bed and drew her into his arms. The trembling wouldn't ease for long minutes until he rubbed her back. Later, when the doctor determined she'd be better off at home for the time being, Jax helped her dress in a gown the hospital provided and disposable panties she never knew they had. Too tired to be embarrassed, she said nothing to Jax the whole time, and he finished up by pulling socks with rubber on the bottom onto her feet.

Tae did complain when he insisted he carry her from the wheelchair to his car, but he disregarded her protests and tucked her in. By the time they got back to her apartment, she fell in and out of sleep, and he tucked her into her own bed. Sometime later, voices woke her, and she strained to hear who it was in her living room. She picked up Jax, Zerita, and Daniel's voices.

"We can take turns caring for her, if you want, but there's not going to be anymore arguing, Daniel."

"Who do you think I am that I would risk her baby?" Daniel shot back. When he spoke again, she could tell he'd forced himself to get better control of his temper. "You're right. No fighting."

"Good," Jax said, "and while we're on the subject, I want you both to know. The baby is mine. Yeah, that's right, Daniel. She told me the truth at the hospital, and I've been thinking if she never slept with you, you couldn't have thought he was yours. That means you knew."

Zerita and Daniel must have gasped, but her friend said nothing while Daniel spoke up. "We can discuss this another time."

"We definitely will," Jax said, his tone a dark warning.

Tae didn't realize she'd moaned, but it couldn't have been very loud. Jax appeared at her bedside. His rough hand raised her chin, and thick fingers caught the teardrop at the corner of her eye. "I'm here," was all he said. Her throat closed. She couldn't form words. Over his shoulder, she spotted Daniel and Zerita, both worried. Daniel appeared devastated, and knowing it hurt her to her core. He'd wanted to be her baby's father even if he wasn't the biological one. She knew he'd kept her secret for selfish reasons, but now with her lies, she had made things worse with him and Jax.

The tension between the two men wasn't the only problem though. As Jax shifted his position so he blocked her view of his best friend, she came to an awareness she never saw coming. She loved Jax. He had been by her side from day one and worked his way into her heart. He cared. That much was obvious, but it didn't mean he was in love with her or that he would commit himself to only her.

"Tae, get some rest, and I'll come by tonight to see you, after work," Daniel said. His familiar voice rolled over her, bringing memories of his intimate touch to the foreground of her mind again. Feelings for him had never died, and she knew even without Jax reaffirming it Daniel still loved her.

"Okay," she said, lowering her gaze so Jax wouldn't read the emotion in her eyes. "Thanks for coming by." Her words sounded too formal, but she had no idea how else to be.

Zerita nudged Jax aside, and he moved now that Daniel had left. She bent down to kiss Tae's cheek. "Hey, girl. I know you and that little fighter are going to be okay. I've already spoken to the boss lady and let her know you need a few days. When and only when you're up to it, give her a call about how long you will be out. Got it?"

"Yes, ma'am." Tae grinned and smirked. "You're bossy."

"I love you. Between all of us, we're going to make sure you get stronger, and if I have to later, I will beat yo' ass."

Tae snickered. Zerita almost never fell into what the woman called "lazy speak."

"Okay, Mama. I got you."

"You better."

Zerita left, and Jax saw her out. When he returned, he brought a tray with food and a glass of grape juice, Tae's favorite. She went to sit up, but he tsked frowning and shaking his head. "Lay still until I get you."

"I'm not an invalid, Jax."

"I thought we agreed you would obey me."

"Doesn't sound familiar."

"You've been warned."

She laughed as he set the tray down on foldable legs and sat beside her. His strong hands gripped her waist, and he hoisted her to a sitting position, then fluffed pillows behind her back.

"If you try to feed me, we're going to fight," she told him.

He grinned but placed the tray on her lap and let her help herself. Tae tucked into the bacon and eggs and toast, a treat since she'd been eating oatmeal and fruit for a while in an effort to be healthy.

"Are we off my diet?" she asked him.

He fingered a bit of honey from the side of her mouth and licked it from his finger. Her thighs should have caught on fire she rubbed together so hard.

"No, I thought the bacon would put you in your happy place."

She grinned. "You know me well."

The smoldering look threw her off balance, but he left the room before she begged him to forget everything and just make love to her. While she finished her food, the phone at her bedside buzzed, and she reached for it. A text message. She slid her finger across the surface of the phone to unlock it and retrieved the messages. Her heart stuttered in her chest at Daniel's name.

"I'll do everything I can for you, Tae. Just please, don't write me off. I love you, and I'll see you soon."

Jax returned and nabbed her phone from her fingers. She tensed thinking he would see the message from Daniel, but he simply laid it on the nightstand and cleared up the tray. "Lay back. Get some sleep. I'll be here all day."

He started out of the room.

"Jax?"

He stopped.

"Are you mad at me?" She hated how she sounded—like a child looking for validation.

He faced her and approached to sit on the bed. "I'm not

123

saying I'm not mad, but… I feel like if this didn't happen you never would have told me about the baby. Tae, he or she is mine. *Mine*. Thinking you were going to let Daniel raise him and let my child call him daddy… That kills me."

Pain glimmered in his eyes, and she hated herself. She touched his face, and he covered her hand to kiss her fingers. Why didn't he tell her to go fuck herself? She deserved it.

"I wouldn't have done that. I know it's easy to say now, but I intended to tell you. There's no way I would let the baby call Daniel daddy and leave you out in the cold."

His disbelief radiated off of him. "I get it. Daniel is successful, the vice president of his company. He's got money on top of money, and while I don't do so bad, I can't touch his bank account."

"You know I don't care about money. I'm not asking either of you for anything."

"Well you're going to get it!" He blew out a heavy breath. "If it makes you feel better, I will get a nine to five."

Her eyes widened. "Jax." *That's not what I want. What do I want?*

"Your job is dangerous, and it scares me to think of you getting killed on an assignment, but you love investigations, and I don't want to take that away from you. My dishonesty had nothing to do with how much money you make or your business."

"It has to do with how much you love Daniel."

She opened her mouth to deny it, but he patted her hand and stood up.

"We're not going to argue. I'm Daddy." His brows hung low, and his mouth was drawn into a straight line. She grinned and nodded. "Now rest. I'm going to take care of a few quick errands, including packing a bag."

"A-A bag?"

"Yes, you have me as a roommate." He kissed her. "Later."

He disappeared out the door, leaving her rattled to her core.

Chapter Thirteen

Tae stood in front of the mirror and stared at her protruding belly. The thing was massive at six months, but she loved it. She loved her baby, and funny enough, she didn't mind her body one bit. Even her heavy breasts pleased her for some reason. Okay, that might be because Jax looked at them like they were lunch, but still, they were nice, and they didn't leak too much.

She heard a noise at the front of the apartment and went to investigate. Jax stood with his back to her, grocery bags at his feet, and she crept up behind him intending to scare him. Maybe being stuck in the apartment was getting to her. Just before she shouted boo, she noticed him frowning down at the stack of mail in his hand. One letter addressed to him read "Past Due" at the bottom of the envelope. He'd spent way too much time looking after her rather than working, and she knew for a fact from overhearing him on the phone that he hadn't taken the higher-paying jobs because they were also more dangerous.

Instead of trying to scare him, she wrapped her arms around his waist and leaned her face against his back. "I'm sorry, Jax. I feel like I'm keeping you from what you need to do."

He tossed the mail aside and turned to take her into his arms. "Never mind. Our budget is fine. I just forgot to pay that bill."

"I don't believe you."

He kissed her. "Your job is to incubate our son, and mine is to look after you."

"I'm no longer on bed rest, you know." She hadn't been for three weeks, and in all that time she hadn't seen Daniel more than once. He never called or texted. Jax had told her Daniel asked after her but nothing more. So did he take back the declaration he made on her phone? She didn't contact him because she wasn't sure if he and Alise were back together. Then again, she figured if they were, Jax would be only too happy to tell her.

He released her and walked into the kitchen with the bags. Jax cooked at her place and stayed the night more often than not. They were practically roommates, but he slept on the couch. He'd told her he wouldn't join her in bed unless she invited him. That didn't stop the man from walking around the apartment in nothing but boxers, showing off his tight body. What made him more impressive was he'd learned to cook well.

"What's with the whipped cream?" she asked when he brought it out. "Mm, and strawberries."

He wiggled his eyebrows at her, and she laughed. "Nothing dirty…unless you want it." His gaze lowered to her breasts, and she chewed the inside of her cheek. If he only knew. "I'm making strawberry shortcake. I found the recipe the other day, and it's simple. Plus, my dad is coming on Friday."

"Say what?"

He shrugged. "We agreed we would finally inform our families, and you're the one that reneged on the decision."

"I didn't renege. I just haven't gotten around to it."

"Hm." He guided her into a chair with no arguments. "Well, my dad is coming to see you."

"You didn't tell him…" She let her words fade away, and he eyed her. The napkin holder in the center of the table seemed much more interesting to examine.

"I didn't say you're mine, although I wanted to."

Her heart did a wild tattoo. She changed the subject. "I've been wanting to take a bath to soak out some of my aches and pains, but I'm kind of scared of getting stuck in there."

"You should have told me. We'll get you in the bath after dinner."

Too late she realized that meant he had to see her naked. Not that she was shy about her body now, funny enough, but being naked in front of Jax tempted her beyond reason. The doctor gave her the go-ahead for sex, and Jax knew it. He would probably try to seduce her.

"Okay."

All through dinner, Tae squirmed. The more she thought of enjoying a bubble bath, she added Jax to it in her mind, and their antics led to other things. She shook her head to dislodge the thoughts, but that did nothing. When she finished eating, Jax sent her off to gather the toiletries she needed and to run the bath water while he cleaned up the kitchen. She stripped off her clothing and put on a bathrobe and slippers. Neither was sexy. The terry cloth robe made her hips look wider, and the footwear swallowed her feet but did not minimize the thick ankles. She stood in the bathroom laughing at herself.

"What's funny?"

She started at the sound of his deep voice and glanced up. The tent in his pants caught her off guard, and she followed his gaze to where she'd let the robe gape and show off her cleavage. "Nothing. What are you looking at?"

"Something," he teased.

She dropped the robe on the floor and stepped out of the slippers. Jax let out an agonized moan. "Get under those bubbles before I forget my vow."

She let him take her arm and guide her over to the side of the tub. "What vow?"

"Don't play dumb, Tae. You know what you're doing to me."

Settling in the water, she ran her hands over her breasts and then cupped her palms to rain water on the swollen mounds. As liquid dripped from her rather large nipples, Jax hissed between his teeth.

"Call me when you're ready to get out."

"Wait, I…" She swung her arm wide, slinging water all over his kaki slacks, right at the crotch. "Oops."

"You're going to pay for that."

She raised her eyebrows. "How? I'm preggo. You can't spank me."

His eyes narrowed. "No, not yet."

She shivered and then squeaked in alarm when he began stripping off his clothes. "What are you doing?"

"You've wet my clothes. I can't stand around in these. I might catch a cold."

"Yeah, right. That's your reason."

"Yup."

He unbelted his buckle, and she licked her lips and swallowed. Muscular legs with a dusting of dark hair over them came into view. The wet pants hit the floor, and he heeled off his shoes. When he raised his arms over his head to pull off his shirt, her gaze locked on his chest. No man should be that delicious-looking. Then again they all should but not in her bathroom when she meant to keep her hands to herself. Okay, who was she kidding? She'd hoped to provoke him, and it had worked.

Leaning back, she ran her hands over her breasts once again and closed her eyes sighing. The tiny moan evoked a groan from him, and she yelped to find him climbing into the tub. "There's not enough room. You're too big," she complained.

Water sloshed over the sides and wet the floor.

"You're going to sit on my lap and help me with a little problem I have."

"What problem is that?" She glanced over to the pile of clothes on the floor and spotted his boxers topping the heap. All kinds of visions popped into her head of his erection.

"This one." He raised her as if she weighed nothing and positioned himself behind her. When he brought her down on his lap, his hard dick slipped between her legs and grazed her pussy. Another moan escaped her lips.

"Jax."

His hands came around and settled on her swollen belly. "You know you want it."

She panted. "Jax, the last time we had sex, it was so rough. I—"

"You can't take it like that now, but after you have our son, I will give you time to heal, and then I'm going to take you like you need to be taken."

Her pussy clenched, and she squeezed her legs together, forgetting she'd trapped his cock between them. That served to heighten her lust. No turning back now. "But I have needs right now."

"And I will not leave you burning." His hands came up to cup her breasts. She gasped and arched into his touch. At his thumbs scraping across her sensitive nipples, she shivered and covered his hands, guiding him in the way she wanted it. He already knew, of course, by the way he pinched the pebbled buds and rolled them with gentle care. They ached but felt so good, and a bit of milk leaked out onto his fingers. Jax moaned, watching. He raised his coated thumb to his mouth and licked it. "Good."

"You're dirty." Her voice came out raspy.

"I'm hungry."

"For more milk?"

"For your pussy. Right here." He squeezed the head of his dick and pressed it to her thigh. "Hold onto the sides of the tub. I'm going to lift you onto it."

"How do you know I'm ready?"

"Aren't you?"

She first touched the head of his cock, loving its warmth and the smooth, rubbery skin. Forcing herself past it, she reached farther down between her legs, and her fingers dipped below water level. They sank without hindrance into her as she was so wet from seeing him naked and having him under her. She bought her hand up, and Jax captured it, touching his fingers to hers. He nuzzled her neck, his voice a low rumble.

"What you do to me, Tae. I've been patient."

"I know."

"I won't be now."

Her breath was a shudder as she drew it in.

He grasped her hips and lifted her. She held onto the sides of the tub, and he arched his hips. As if her pussy gave off a homing beacon, his shaft found her entrance and sank wonderfully inside, stretching her walls, so long without a man's use. Her mouth fell open, and even before he'd filled her to capacity, she wriggled her hips, grinding on him. Air hissed between Jax's teeth, and his fingers dug into her sides. He tightened his hold to slow her down. They moved as one, coming together and her arching up so his cock slid out, then back together again.

"Do you have any idea how bad I've wanted you, woman, and how good it feels to be inside you?"

More water splashed over the side of the tub as she grabbed his hands to try to push them away. She wanted to bounce hard until she lost her mind. Even with Jax controlling the speed at which they moved, the noises she made escalated. Her pussy throbbed, and her clit surely couldn't swell any more. He grazed it each time he drove into her, and she couldn't take it.

"I know," she moaned. "Let go, Jax. I want it hard, please."

"Easy, honey. I can't let go, but I'm going to give you what you want." He slid his hands from her waist to her legs and raised them. One of her heels on the tub's edge, she felt a scream bubbling in her throat and fell onto Jax's chest. He withdrew until just the head of his cock penetrated her pussy and then drove up, slow and gentle. At the same time, he slid a hand up her inner thigh until he reached her clit and ran the pad of a thumb over it.

The pitch to her whine rose a few decibels. How did he always make her scream? What was it about his touch? She lost track of that train of thought when her apex began to tingle and her core muscles contracted. "I'm…going…to…come…" She panted and pushed at his hand on her clit. Jax massaged her bud faster. "Jax, stop I can't take it. Too good."

"Never," he growled in her ear. "You're going to come for me right now. That's your punishment."

She screamed his name and found herself riding both his cock and his fingers. Her breasts bounced heavy on her protruding belly, and her nipples hurt, but the pain didn't detract from the pleasure. She rocked her hips faster. Jax kept a thumb on her clit and pushed two fingers atop his cock as it impaled her.

"Come on, baby, give me your sweet come. You know how I like to eat your pussy, don't you? Ride my cock."

The dirty talk and the pumping inside her did it. She screamed over and over as an orgasm exploded through her being, but before her climax could die down, a pounding started on the front door. She squealed in fear, and Jax slapped a hand over her mouth.

Tae froze. Her eyes widened, and she looked at the sodden floor. Had the water leaked into the downstairs apartment? The pounding started up again, and Jax raised her up out of the tub and set her on her feet. He didn't release her until he stepped out of the tub as well and marched the two of them out of the bathroom onto the safer surface of the carpet.

When Jax opened the bedroom door, she picked up the voice of her neighbor more clearly. "Tae, are you okay? I heard screaming. Tae?"

Tae could have sunk through the floor. The neighbor wasn't the one downstairs but the one next door. She'd been too loud. "This is your fault, Jax."

He seemed unrepentant and threw on a pair of pants as headed to the front door. Embarrassed, Tae hid in the walk-in closet as if her neighbor would barge into her apartment and demand to see proof she wasn't dying. She did all she could not to hear the details of the two men's conversation because something told her Jax would not cover the truth of what they had been up to.

"You can stop hiding now. He's gone."

She glared at him. "I'm not hiding. I was just looking for something to put on."

He shook his head and snagged her wrist to pull her forward. "Oh no, you're not putting anything on. I'm not done with you."

Her curiosity got the better of her. "What did you tell him?"

"I told him you were riding my cock."

She yelped. "Tell me you didn't say that."

He chuckled and turned her to the bed. "Lie down and wait for me while I clean up the water in the bathroom."

"Jax."

He ignored her call and disappeared. She ground her teeth, but she knew no amount of nagging the man would get him to admit anything. Jax was blunt and crazy. He probably did say it, and now she'd have to see her neighbor's red face every time she ran into him. *Great. Thanks, Jax.*

A few minutes later, he returned from the bathroom, and she took him in from head to foot. "Why do you have so many clothes on?"

He grinned. "A pair of pants? Not even boxers under here." He ran a hand over his crotch, igniting her between the legs with such a move.

"Like I said, too much material." She curled a finger, signaling him over.

His brows rose. "You want this here?"

"You know I do."

"Are you sure?" He undid his pants and let them gape open, revealing that he'd already gone hard again or never softened to begin with. She bit her bottom lip, staring. Jax wasn't as thick as Daniel, but he did have a good span and length, and boy oh boy did he know how to use his equipment. She forgot to answer, and he pulled his cock free of his pants to stroke it in his palm. His voice when he spoke had dropped lower. "Tell me you want it, Tae."

She shivered. "I do."

"Say it again."

"I want your cock, Jax."

"Where."

"In my—"

"Show me," he demanded.

A lump rose in her throat at his rough tone. She rose to her knees and turned away from him then touched her ass cheek.

"Tae," he warned.

She moved her fingers to her rear entrance and shut her eyes. His moan sent ripples of awareness over her skin.

"Good girl. Now lie down on your side."

She obeyed. Jax walked out of the room, and she heard him rummaging around in the living room where he'd left his overnight bag. When he returned, he held a condom packet and a tube of K-Y Jelly. Tae squirmed in anticipation. Jax climbed on the bed and tore open the packet. She watched as he rolled it down his cock. She reached for it, but he pushed her hand away, making a clicking sound. When he repositioned one her legs forward and bent it at the knee, he leaned over and kissed the back of her thigh. A swipe of his tongue along the delicate skin made her shiver and murmur encouragement.

"Oh, I have every intention of continuing," he said between sucking her skin and laving it as he made his way higher. "You belong to me, but you're not ready to acknowledge it yet."

"Jax…"

He pushed her butt cheeks apart, and she jammed her face into the pillow. Jax didn't do what she feared he would do. He pushed a greased finger into her anus and began working it around in a circle. The pressure from his entrance and movements robbed her of thought. She stuffed the comforter into her mouth. Still her moan erupted.

"Looks like somebody likes what I'm doing to her," Jax teased. He eased his finger deeper and then pulled it out. Tae struggled for a breath. The sensations overwhelmed her. She reached back and grabbed his wrist. He made a reprimanding sound. "You know better. Move the hand, or I won't give you any more."

"Jax."

"Now, Tae."

She balled both hands in the covers and buried her face. He added a second finger, and she thought she'd faint. Her head spun, her pussy throbbed, and another orgasm began to build. He knew how he tortured her. He was mean and wonderful at the same time, tough and cruel. She arched into his exploration and whimpered his name. In her mind, she begged him, but she knew to say it out aloud would get her more punishment. Jax would not be rushed.

At long last, he penetrated her anus with three fingers, but he didn't leave them in long. He pulled out and replaced the digits with his cock. The head squeezed past her tight entrance with much prodding. This wasn't the first time she'd been taken from behind, but it robbed her of lucidity nonetheless. Jax scooted close, spooning her ass. He tossed an arm over her shoulder and across her chest. His big palm engulfed one of her breasts, and then he thrust forward. His cock sank to the hilt. She opened her mouth to scream and found it covered with Jax's other hand. Her cries muffled, she started to play with her clit while he ground into her ass. Her climax descended like a storm, tearing through her body, rocking her world. She pushed back on Jax's cock and rode him as fast as he would allow. This time no one interrupted while her lover found his release.

"Ah, Tae, what you do," he whispered in her ear when he was done.

"Not my fault."

"Who dropped their robe in the bathroom?"

"Who walked in there with a hard-on?"

"No idea."

She laughed, and he squeezed her in a hug. When he pulled out and discarded the used condom, she moaned. He looked at her. "I can take you again if you like."

"A little rest?"

He leaned over and kissed her lips. Her heart beat faster with love for him.

"Of course. Take a nap. I'm going to get cleaned up."

She yawned. "Okay." Before she even got the words out, she began to drift off, but for the second time someone knocked at the door. Tae looked at Jax, and he shrugged. At least the person wasn't banging like they'd lost their mind. Jax had muffled her screams, so it couldn't be because she'd been too loud. The doorbell rang. She sat up. "I'll get it."

"No. You're resting."

She slid to the end of the bed. "Go clean up, Jax. I'm fine."

After locating her second favorite robe, one thinner and less comfy than the terry cloth, she headed to the front door. She yawned again before she reached it, putting a hand up to her mouth. Exhaustion came over her so she wasn't thinking straight when she pulled open the door without first checking the peephole. The woman standing with her back turned made Tae curse herself for her stupidity.

Janita spun to face her. "Sis, I'm here for a loan. I'm not even hearing your excus—" Her eyes bugged as she took in Tae's belly. "What the hell? Are you pregnant?"

Tae readjusted her robe. "Fat."

She spun away from the door and headed into the living room, her sister tumbling after her. The door slammed, making Tae wince.

"Don't you lie to me. You're knocked up! Who's the fucker that did it? Does Ma know? Wait, of course not or she would have told me. I'm calling her."

"Janita!" Tae faced her sister, frustrated and worried to see her whipping out her cell phone, a phone that seemed to be in perfect working order with no sign of cracks as Janita had been texting her about for months now. "I'll tell her my news myself."

Janita smirked. "When your baby is in college?"

"What do you care?"

Her sister paused in the act of dialing and placed a hand over her chest. "I'm your sister. If I'm hurt because you didn't tell me, what do you think Ma will feel?"

Tae folded her arms over her chest. "You're not hurt. You're calculating how much you'll lose by me having another mouth to feed."

"Can you blame me? You've always been there for me, Tae, and now I see why you left me hanging all these months."

"So selfish of me to have my own life and responsibilities."

Janita rolled her eyes. "You always claimed you didn't want kids. I should have known it was a lie. You thought you were better than us."

"You know what, Janita, I'm sick of the attitude. I don't owe you anything."

"Tae."

She turned and glared at Jax. "Don't dare to tell me to calm down."

"You should." He strode up and glanced meaningfully at her belly. "Nothing is worth our son's life. No *one* is."

Janita sneered. "Another white man? Damn, don't you like your own kind anymore?"

Tae clenched her hands into fists and released them over and over. She wanted to wrap her fingers around her sister's throat and wring her neck until she shut up. "Who I date isn't your business, and you claim not to have any money, but here you are in Charlotte. Jersey is a long way away."

"I took a bus, okay? Besides, that's not the point." She hesitated, and Tae was taken aback when her sister burst out crying. "I left Terry!"

Both Tae and Jax stood there in shock for a few minutes, staring at Janita and not knowing what to do. Tae knew her sister, and she would not leave her moneymaker unless she had another lined up. She did like drama and to be the center of attention, but Tae didn't want to jump to conclusions unless Janita really was hurting. She loved her. She just couldn't stand her for long periods.

Tae rubbed her side, and when Jax glanced at her, she dropped her hand and approached her sister to try to get her to stop with the loud hiccupping sobs. *Is she five, for goodness sakes?*

The doorbell rang, and Tae groaned. Not another person. Janita wasn't so loud the neighbors needed to get involved. Jax beat her to the door and opened it. Tae blinked at finding Terrence, Janita's husband standing there. Had all of New Jersey traveled south? She peered over her brother-in-law's shoulder but saw no one else in the hall.

"Is Janita here?" Terrence demanded, like he didn't see her making a scene in the middle of the living room.

Janita whirled around, pausing in her performance—or preparing for a new scene in it. "What are you doing here, Terry?"

The new drama unfolding before Tae as her sister and brother-in-law argued and then made up then back to arguing drove Tae to the brink. Jax seemed ready to throttle the couple and throw her over his shoulder to force her into the bedroom. She shouted at him that she was fine and so was the baby. The nightmare only escalated. Then the front door opened again. With an expression of serenity, Daniel took in the scene and no doubt came to his own conclusions.

"Terrence and Janita." Daniel's voice rose above the din, and all of a sudden silence reigned. "Good to see you two again."

Janita's brows rose. "You're seeing two men, sis? Damn."

Tae rolled her eyes. "Funny how you came to that conclusion."

Terrence shook Daniel's hand, and they passed a few words between them. Daniel dug into his pocket and brought out his wallet. He peeled off a few bills from a thick wad of cash. "Let me buy you two dinner."

Terrence held up his hands. "That's not nece—"

Janita snatched the money and began counting it. "Thanks. Come on, Terry. We'll see you later, Tae."

Two minutes after Tae exhaled in relief that her family was gone, her cell phone rang. She looked at the display to see that it was her mother calling. The muscles of her stomach clenched. She knew without a doubt Janita had wasted no time to tell her mother she was pregnant.

She moaned, her finger hovering above the Connect button.

Daniel crossed the room and slipped the phone from her fingers. She stared as he answered. "Mrs. Croft, how are you? This is Daniel. Yes, I'm well. Thanks. Sure. I understand. That's kind of what I wanted to talk to Tae about today."

Tae's mouth hung open. What the heck were they discussing? She reached for the phone, but Daniel turned his back and disappeared into the kitchen. Glancing at Jax turned out to be a mistake. His face looked like a thundercloud.

"Why does he think it's his right to talk to your mother?" he growled. "This has nothing to do with him."

"As if I know?"

Her mood shot, Tae stomped into the bedroom and headed to the bathroom to take a shower. By the time she returned decent, both men sat in her living room talking as if it was not awkward having them there together. She didn't know whether to sit beside Daniel, who had parked on the couch, or lean on the arm of the chair Jax occupied. She paused, tugging on the dress she wore, feeling like Daniel could tell just by looking what Jax and she had done earlier.

Daniel stood up. "Tae, your mom is expecting your call, but for now, I was wondering if you'd take a drive with me."

"It's getting late," Jax snapped.

She looked from him to Jax. The living room never shrank so fast. From Jax's outburst and expression, he didn't like the invitation, but he didn't fight to keep her there. She did want to talk to Daniel, to ask where he'd been and if everything was okay at home. Most of all, she'd missed him and just wanted to hear his voice. "Um, sure. Hang on a sec."

Their low murmurs reached her as she went back into her room, and she smiled to herself at Jax's insistence that Daniel not let her overdo it wherever they went. Daniel's "I'll take care of her," warmed Tae's heart, and she hurried to get her sweater.

Chapter Fourteen

I filed for divorce."

Tae gaped at Daniel as he sat in his car in a grocery store parking lot. "You what?"

He reached for her hand and laced fingers with hers. Her heart raced out of control. When he massaged her skin with his thumb, she swallowed and looked away.

"I can't pretend anymore, Octavia. I care about Alise, but I was fooling myself thinking I was in love with her. I thought somehow going through with marrying her would erase you from my heart. I was wrong, and I wasn't being fair to her or myself. I won't stay in a relationship that is doomed to fail because I can't stop loving you."

Tears welled up in her eyes and spilled down her cheeks. "I don't know what to say."

"Tell me you don't love me."

She gasped.

"Say I have no chance with you."

"Will you go back to Alise?"

"No."

She eased her fingers from his and clutched hers together in her lap. "It's wrong, Daniel. I feel bad like I destroyed your marriage. I can't be the other woman."

He frowned. "So you're going to throw away what we could have because of guilt?"

"It's not that simple."

"Explain it to me!" He grunted and ran fingers through his hair. "I'm sorry. I shouldn't have yelled at you."

"You call that yelling?"

He shrugged.

"I love Jax too," she whispered.

He looked like she'd punched him in the gut.

"I'm sorry."

"You said 'too.' That means you still love me."

She could have kicked herself. "Daniel, I feel like I'm in a tug-of-war. I can't deal with this."

"I'm sorry, baby." She thought he'd back off, but he grabbed her chin and turned her head to face him. The inches between them disappeared. "I'm not backing down. I stayed away long enough. I love you, and I'm *going* to have you."

His mouth descended on hers. She scarcely had time to draw in a breath before he claimed her lips in a searing kiss. He forced her lips apart and snaked his tongue into her mouth. Wet panties and hardened nipples were the least of her issues when she brought her hands up to push him away. Instead, her fingers curled into his shirt. While she didn't push him away, she didn't draw him closer either.

Daniel took his time kissing her, tearing down all her defenses and leaving her raw and vulnerable. When he raised his head, her lips were numb and her heart sore. She put a hand to her mouth and stared at the woman struggling with a full cart, pushing it a slight incline to her SUV. Others entered and exited the grocery store, and out at the main road, cars zoomed by. The entire world went about its business while she had come to a screeching, confused halt. Why wasn't it easier than this?

"Marry me."

She shut her eyes. "Daniel."

"I know I got it wrong years ago."

"So you *don't* have a problem with me working?"

"I don't like it, but I just want you to be happy. If a job makes you happy, we can work around it. I just want you with me."

Six months ago she might have jumped in his lap and demanded he take her home to stay. "I can't just walk away from Jax, and I can't have you both."

"You're right about that," he ground out. She looked at him. The bitter anger in his eyes was almost palpable. "The friendship we had won't return to the way it was."

She felt sick.

"The second you choose me, if he touches you, he's dead."

"He's my baby's daddy, Daniel."

"And he will have visitation rights."

She stared. Daniel may have claimed to accept her working, but his words made her feel like nothing had changed. He wanted to control everything. Not that Jax was much different. She didn't blame either man, but neither of them truly understood her position.

"Can you take me home, please? I'm feeling pretty worn out. It's been a long day."

He turned over the car engine. "I hoped we could have a late dinner together."

Right now she had a lot of thinking to do, and who knew what mental condition she'd have after she spoke with her mother. "I already ate, but can I call you tomorrow?"

He seemed disappointed. "Sure."

Tae rode in silence as Daniel drove her back to the apartment. When they arrived, the apartment lay empty, and she found a note Jax left. She skimmed it.

"Okay?" Daniel asked.

She nodded. "Yes, I'm okay. I'm just going to bed."

He hesitated. "Since he's not here…"

"I'm grown, Daniel. I can stay home by myself."

"Call me if you need me."

She thought she heard an emphasis on the word *me*, but let it go. "All right."

Before she could deny him, he dropped a kiss on her lips and walked out the door. She made sure the door was locked and then returned to Jax's note. He sometimes took investigation assignments late at night because that's when most people were off work and Jax could catch them at home. He knew she had a doctor's appointment the next day and promised to be home to take her and pick her up.

"Home, huh?" she muttered. Well it was a good thing he'd gone. She could rest and think about what to do. A buzz from her phone caught her attention, and she checked it. The text came from her sister Sasha.

"Ma is a mess, crying like you killed somebody. Congratulations on the baby. I'm sad you didn't tell me, but I know you. Call your mother before she drives me crazy. I beg you."

A pulse pounded in Tae's head, but she sat down on the couch rather than heed the call of her bed. Now she knew Daniel had been talking to her mother about getting back together with her. The knowledge pissed her off. He didn't need to bring her family into things, but at least he hadn't been the one to tell her mother about the baby. No, the catty Janita had done that.

Her mother had the nerve to wait three rings before she answered the phone. "Hi, Ma, how's it going? I have news for you, even though I'm sure you already know…"

❖

"How did she take it?" Jax asked Tae the next day on the way to the doctor's office.

"Like my mother takes everything—as if I got pregnant to spite her. She feels we should wait to have sex until we're married. My sisters and I, I mean. None of us did, but at least Sasha and Janita waited until they were married before they had kids. So I'm the black sheep. She says I broke her heart."

Jax studied her face in between focusing on the road. "I don't know your mother at all, but I don't want her to upset you. I can talk to her if you need me to."

"No way, Jax. You'd make it worse. I can hear you now telling her if she is going to upset me, she'll have to wait until after the baby is born to talk to me again."

He frowned, and his grip on the steering wheel tightened. "That's what you think of me? That I only care about our son, and your mom can verbally abuse you all she wants after he's born? I suppose you think Daniel would charm her."

She groaned. "Don't start."

"What did the two of you talk about last night?"

"Are you going to tell me about the job you took?" She wondered if he'd rushed out to take one after seeing how Daniel had settled the craziness with Janita and Terrence by giving them money. Janita had texted her later that Daniel had given them enough for gas back home. She'd even gone so far as to insist if Tae had to marry a white man it should be Daniel. Tae had no trouble seeing a future of Janita constantly trying to dig into Daniel's pocket with that scenario. Of course she would put a stop to it. *What am I thinking? Like I'm going to accept his proposal.*

"Tae."

She snapped out of her reverie. "What? I didn't hear you."

Jax eyed her. "You wanted to know about the case I took, but you're not listening."

"I'm sorry." She laid a hand on his arm and slid fingers down to his hand. Today, Jax wore his usual when he intended to work, a dress shirt and dark slacks. The burgundy-and-white pinstripe looked good on him, and she planned to get him a few more from Brooks Brothers since his birthday was in a few weeks. He would turn thirty-five.

"Tae, you're still not listening."

"Sorry!" She squeaked in alarm. "I was thinking about your birthday and what we'll do."

He smiled. "We don't have to do anything."

"We can afford something, Jax. All our money is going to bills and savings, but you've been good to me. I want to do something special."

Tension around his mouth worried her, but he turned his hand face up to link with hers. Then he drew hers to his mouth to kiss. "We'll talk about it later. I have to check out a few things while you're at the doc, so this time I'm not staying, but I'll be back to pick you up, okay?"

She sighed. "Okay."

"Tae?"

"What?"

"You're really fine with it?"

"I know you have to work, Jax. You've spent too much time at my side and neglected work."

"With you is where I belong. In fact, I was doing some thinking."

Her stomach fluttered, and she suspected it had more to do with nerves rather than the baby kicking.

"What would you say about us combining households? Your

apartment is good, but you know I have my house. It's small but big enough for the three of us."

She faced the street ahead of them. "The commute—"

"Is only an extra ten miles, not that big a deal."

"I know."

The fact was he didn't tell her he loved her. She wasn't sure if Jax saying it would make everything perfect. Letting go of Daniel didn't feel possible yet.

"Can I think about it?"

He sighed. "Okay, but don't take too long."

"Or what?"

He smirked. "Nothing. Just don't."

She rolled her eyes. "Yes, Mr. Hart."

A few minutes later, Jax dropped her off. Tae moved to get out of the car, but he grabbed her hand. "Hey, where are you going?"

She paused. "What do you mean?"

He pointed to his lips. The lower, full one particularly called to her. "Right here, beautiful."

She couldn't help the grin. Jax, the fun guy, was still in there. "I can't reach," she teased. "The armrest and my belly…"

Jax was out of the car within seconds and jogged around the back until he reached her door. He opened it wide and leaned in. Tae got a whiff of his aftershave, and it made her mouth water. She took in the glimpse of his smooth chest through the opening of his shirt's top button. He'd lain his tie on the back seat, and she knew he'd slip it on at the last minute.

"And what is your excuse now?"

She lowered her lashes. "None."

Jax captured her chin and raised it before slanting his mouth over hers. He parted her lips and slipped his tongue between them. A moan crept up her throat, and she didn't hold it back.

Jax kissed her deeply, drew back just enough to break the connection but not the warmth of his nearness, and then devoured her mouth again. Her nipples ached to feel his touch, and her pussy grew moist. She squirmed in her seat, needing him, until he deemed her good and conquered. Then he straightened.

"Now you can go inside." He held out his hand, and she took it to rise. "Okay?" he asked softly. "I can see you inside."

"I can get there. Thanks."

She managed to walk with some semblance of control to the clinic door and hurried inside. When she looked back through the window, Jax waved, then gunned the engine as he tore out of the parking lot.

Tae moved through the appointment with her thoughts full of both Jax and Daniel. What would she do? What did she want to do? Daniel asked her to marry him, and Jax wanted her to move in with him. The decision should be simple, but she loved them both. Each man had positives and negatives about him. Jax was a lot of fun, and sex with him blew her mind to pieces. His rough touch although without sophistication gave her life sometimes. Then there was the fact that his job was dangerous, and if he pulled back from it even a little, he didn't make enough money. Just asking him to ease up in the first place made her feel guilty. She loved her career just as much as he loved his.

Daniel had money. That was not an issue with him. He'd paid his dues and moved up the corporate ladder. He took life a lot more seriously than Jax did, but that didn't mean she didn't enjoy being with him. She did. His gentle touch pleasured her and made her feel cherished. She had no doubt she would always come first in his life, and he had already proven he loved her. The man had married a woman who looked like her for goodness sake, but he loved her so much he couldn't let go and make his marriage work. Guilt rode her because of it even while his actions solidified his feelings. The problem with Daniel was he wanted her at home with his little one. He might claim he would be flexible, but would he? Daniel desired that old-fashioned family dream with white picket fence and a wife who baked cookies and joined the PTA. He might be willing to put that dream aside, but would it make him happy in the long run? Could they overcome their different views of what they wanted in life?

"Ms. Croft, we're all done. You can get dressed now."

Tae blinked and glanced down at her belly. The technician hadn't completely wiped away the gel she used when administering the sonogram. Tae took the offered tissue and cleaned up herself then worked her way off the table. "Can I go to the bathroom before that? I'm about to burst."

The woman smiled. "Of course. We've all been there. Across the hall, second door."

Tae had been to the clinic a million times. She knew where the bathroom was but made no comment as she dashed as fast her as swollen ankles and rounded belly would allow. Once she handled her business and had washed her hands, she returned to the room but paused long enough to call Jax before she got dressed. After four rings, the phone went to voice mail. She frowned and typed a text message.

I'm ready. Please come now. I'm starving.

She dressed and went through the mundane procedure of checking out. Jax still hadn't called or texted. When she stepped out of the clinic, she searched the parking lot for him, but saw no sign of his car. "Damn it. I could have driven myself, but he insisted. So over this."

At least she didn't have to go into to the office. Incredible favor allowed her to work part time in the office and part time at home. Tae considered it a miracle. She might not be on bed rest, but the doctor insisted on little stress. That was the only reason she'd gotten the special treatment, another reason she loved her job.

She checked her purse. No cash. Across the street was a Harris Teeter and a couple restaurants. She could grab something to eat and get some money for the bus. Frowning, she wondered if the CATS bus schedule might be easily accessible on her cell phone. *Stupid Jax.*

Then she remembered that Jax never forgot her or missed her appointments. She recalled what happened the last time he stood her up, and all thought of eating disappeared. He might be somewhere hurt and unable to call. What if it was worse this time? What if he was dead?

She cried out, and clutched her stomach, tears spilling down her cheeks. A man who had been strolling to his car turned around, saw her, and rushed over. "Are you having the baby? What do we do? Call the police? Somebody help!"

Tae fought to get control. She willed her breathing to slow so she didn't hyperventilate, but the pain of Jax being hurt bore heavy on her emotions. "No, please," she panted. "Don't. I'm fine. I just need to sit down."

She wound up back in the doctor's office, a cup of water in her hand, and a nurse taking her vitals.

"Really, I'm okay," she insisted.

"Can't be too careful, Ms. Croft. You're only seven months. Did something happen after you left?"

She refused to admit her fears. "No."

"Well, Dr. Chen doesn't want you leaving on your own. Is Mr. Hart picking you up?"

She almost burst out crying at the mention of his name and the fact that they knew him well enough to know he was always with her. "I'm going to call my…other friend. He'll be here soon."

"Okay." The nurse rubbed her back and straightened. "I'll be back in a few minutes. Dr. Chen will want to talk to you again. You stay right there, and when your friend gets here, he'll need to come inside to get you."

Tae stared down at her phone with the favorites on screen. She hesitated over Daniel's shortcut, remembering him asking her to call him if she needed him. Then she moved on to Zerita's number and pressed that. The phone rang several times and went to voice mail. She hung up and called Zerita's office line. Her friend's assistant picked up.

"Zerita Fox's desk. This is Pamela. May I help you?"

"Hey, Pam. Is Zerita around?"

"Hi, Mommy. How's it going?"

Tae gritted her teeth. Pam's teasing was the last thing she felt like dealing with at this time. "Fine. Is she there? It's kind of important."

"Nope, sorry. She's in another endless meeting. I don't know how she gets writing done, but don't tell them I said so."

"I won't." Tae ended the call with a few assurances that she would keep everyone updated on herself and the baby. She dialed Daniel. *Jax is fine. Jax is fine.*

"Baby?" Daniel breathed into the phone. His gentle tone unleashed the floodgates. She cried like a fool, blubbering incomprehensible words. Even as she noted the sympathetic glances from the nurses and confused annoyance from a few patients passing by, she couldn't quite pull herself together.

"Where are you?" Daniel managed to break through the onslaught.

"At the clinic."

"I'm on my way."

He disconnected the line without another word. All she could do was sit there and wait, holding on to the hope that her baby's daddy was fine. Twenty minutes later, she'd already spoken with the doctor again, and Daniel walked through the door where Tae waited. He paused just inside the entrance, and she would have signaled to him, but stupid emotions overcame her. He scanned the area, spotted her, and then headed over. When he stooped to touch her cheek, she cried some more like an idiot. Daniel drew her into his arms and rubbed her back. He asked nothing while she sobbed it out.

"Oh good, your friend is here," the chipper nurse said. "Mr…?"

Daniel stood up and drew her to her feet to tuck her close to his side. "Daniel Elliott. Is it okay to take her home?"

"Yes, definitely. Dr. Chen spoke with her. Looks like it's just emotional. Pregnant women get that way sometimes. Everything seems to overwhelm us, especially in the last trimester. Please, be kind to her and let her deal with it her own way. Call us if you need anything, Ms. Croft."

Tae ducked her head. Embarrassment kept her mute. Daniel led her to the front of the clinic and out to where he'd parked. She pretended to fall asleep while they rode back to her apartment, but when he saw her inside, he confronted her.

"What's gong on, Octavia?"

"Don't talk like that," she snapped.

He drew her to the couch and placed pressure on her shoulders until she gave in and sat down. She tried to draw away when he took her hands, but he held on. "Talk to me, baby."

"Please, Daniel."

"I can't help if you don't talk to me."

She sniffed and looked at him. "Why didn't Jax pick me up? Is he hurt? You can tell me the truth."

Daniel looked away from her and then hesitated. "He's not hurt. He and I were talking. He didn't want me to tell you but…"

Her heart constricted.

"He can't look after you the way you need. He intended to talk to you tonight—"

"What do you mean he can't look after me? I'm not a fucking child!"

"Tae."

She jerked her hands out of his. "Get out. I'm going to rest. You did your good deed. Now you can go. I've been letting you two act like nursemaids, vying for my attention all these months. Well that ends today. Jax should have manned up and told me this was all too much and he was pulling out." Her voice wobbled, but she cleared her throat. "He just asked… Never mind. I want you to go, Daniel."

He stood up as well. "I can stay."

"No, I'm working from home today, so after my nap I'm going to be editing."

"Have you thought about my proposal?"

She clenched her hands at her sides and spun away from him Putting off telling him about her decision was the last thing she wanted to do, having learned her lesson with Jax. "I'm sorry. I can't marry you."

"You can't, or you won't?" He walked up behind her and turned her around to face him. For the first time, she felt Daniel's strength and saw real anger in his face, directed at her. "Is it because of him? Because it's obvious he doesn't give a damn about you, Tae. He left you stranded at the hospital."

"This has nothing to do with Jax."

"How can I believe that? You fucked him when my back was turned."

She glared at him and wrenched free of his touch. "Excuse me? When your back was turned? I believe you were marrying another woman, and I was not in a relationship with you.

Further more, I'm *still* not. So you can get down off your high horse."

"I already told you, Tae."

She tossed her purse on the couch and then removed her sweater. "Already told me what?"

A finger beneath her chin made her duck away, but Daniel wouldn't be put off. He grabbed her by both arms and drew her closer. For an instant it seemed like he didn't even care that he pressed too hard on her belly. She opened her mouth to tell him where to go, but he covered her mouth with his. Tae punched at his chest, but he caught her hands and pinned them between them. She couldn't get away. Her grunts of protest and squirming in his hold went unheeded, and a slice of fear stole her breath. He released her mouth and rained kisses across her cheek and down her neck.

"I'm not letting you leave me," he whispered in her ear, and a tremor raced down her back. "You love me, and I love you. That should be enough. No, that *will* be enough."

The front door slammed hard, and she jumped. Daniel took his time raising his head from where he nuzzled her neck and turned half-closed, lust filled eyes toward Jax. Tae looked too, and her fear turned to anger. She managed to break from Daniel's hold and charged across the room toward Jax.

"I guess I'm interrupt—" Jax began, but she cracked him across the cheek with an open palm. She drew back to do it again despite how her hand stung, but Jax stopped the attack. He frowned at her. "What the hell is your problem, Tae?"

"What's *my* problem? What's yours? You left me stranded. You didn't call, and you…" She clamped her teeth together. No way was she crying again or showing him how scared she was something had happened. He seemed to see it anyway, her terror and devastation. His strong grip on her wrist turned soft, and he drew her over to the couch to make her sit down. When she did, she didn't look at him, instead blinking rapid fire at the table lamp.

Daniel stood above them, clenching and unclenching his hands. Tae sensed his frustration, but she didn't give a damn at the moment how he felt. He'd forced himself on her, and if she had thought one signal from her would have made him back off, then it wouldn't have been an issue. Daniel had crossed the line.

"Tae, please forgive me. Usually when you have that procedure it lasts another hour."

"So that's your excuse for abandoning me?"

"I didn't abandon you."

"That's not what I got."

Jax cast a glance at Daniel, his expression full of suspicion. "What did he tell you, baby?" He focused back on Tae, and she began to wonder.

"Did you tell Daniel you can't handle me and the baby anymore?"

"Why would I do that when I asked you to move in with me this morning?"

"You did what?" Daniel roared. "Maybe you don't understand the fact that Tae loves me, and you're in the way."

"No, you don't understand. She's mine, and she's carrying *my* baby." Jax jumped to his feet, getting into Daniel's face. They were a close match in height and build, and Tae had seen them fight. She knew the damage both could do.

"Only because you're a lowlife who fucks another man's woman the first chance he gets."

"Stop!" Tae moved between them and faced Daniel. "I need you to leave."

"Me?" He glared over her head at Jax. "What about him?"

"I need to talk to him."

He didn't move.

"Now, Daniel, or do I need to call the police?"

His eyes widened. "Tae, you know—"

"Yes, but I asked you to go. *Please.*"

With slumped shoulders, he crossed to the exit and wrenched open the door. She thought he'd look back at her, but he kept moving and disappeared. The door slammed behind him. Jax's hands came around her waist, but she shoved him away and sat on the couch.

"You've got two minutes to explain to me why you thought ignoring me because usually I take longer at the doctor was fine and dandy. In that time, you explain to me why Daniel told me you're...you..." She coughed, clearing the lump from her throat. "You're leaving me."

Amid her protests, Jax raised her up, sat down, and drew her onto his lap. She beat at his chest, and he let her do it. When he didn't respond and she panted exhausted, she stopped and laid her head on his shoulder.

"I thought you were shot again." A sob escaped her. "I can't do this, Jax."

"I know, baby." He lifted her chin and made her look into his eyes. "That's why I was at a job interview."

She gasped. "A what?"

"First, let me show you this."

A lot of thoughts ran through her mind when he dug into his pocket, and her stomach knotted as she waited. No squeal of delight bubbled up in her throat when Jax brought out his cell phone. She blinked at it and then at him.

His lopsided grin made her want to find a baseball bat.

"It's dead," he explained. "Remember I dropped it on that last case, and I told you the connections were spotty?"

"Yes, you hung up on me a million times."

He chuckled. "I promise I didn't, baby. It's the phone, and

now it won't hold a charge. I was going to take you with me to pick out a new one since this one is crap. I'm so sorry. I thought I had more time. The interview went longer than I expected, and by the time I drove to the clinic you were gone. They told me Daniel picked you up. That one red-headed nurse didn't look too pleased with me dropping the ball like that."

"Yeah, nobody's pleased with you. Least of all me."

"I beg your forgiveness and promise it won't happen again."

"Stop making promises you can't keep."

He held up a finger. "This time I can. I got the job."

"What job?"

"A desk job where I will be safe to come home to my wife and son every night."

"Your what now?" Tae's head swirled, and she thought she might fall over.

Jax stood her on her feet. "Come on. It's time for your afternoon nap, and isn't this your scheduled day for working? Don't want to fall behind. We'll talk at dinner."

She mumbled protests, but he shuffled her along, kissed her forehead, and shut her into the bedroom. Tae cursed him out under breath and decided to accept him putting her off. If he didn't mean what he insinuated, there was no sense in her pushing him to explain. The fact remained that Jax got a regular job for her and their child. The man was one in a million.

Chapter Fifteen

Tae stood in front of the full-length mirror as she often did and examined her body, also the norm. Her belly had dropped considerably, and any day now she would go into labor. The knowledge scared her and excited her at the same time. The bedroom door opened, and Jax strode in. "I forgot what you said to—" He stopped cold, his gaze on her nipples.

Tae rolled her eyes. "You act like you've never see a naked woman before."

"Baby, I see you naked every day, and every day is the first time."

She glanced down and found a tent in his jeans. Men could not fake it. She grinned. "Well stop looking. I just got out of the shower, and you're not going to get me dirty again."

He took a step in her direction. "Are you sure about that?"

She retreated. "I mean it, Jax. You act like a horny teenager."

"Of course. You stopped denying me. I'm making up for lost time. Besides, my job is very hard, and I need a reward."

"Boy please, you head up the Special Investigations Unit at that insurance company. You've got lackeys to do the hard stuff, and they pay you well for it." When Jax had shared the details of his new position and the salary amount, she'd let loose a whistle.

Not only would he do some of the same work he used to do, but it would be steady pay with less danger. In addition to that, he got to train rookies in the field, and they actually looked up to him. The fact that she could tell he was happy in his new position was what did it for her more than anything and took away the guilt.

"Mental anguish from dealing with idiots?" he suggested. "I need your tender loving care."

"Not falling for it."

He went into a long diatribe of why she should give in to his charms while he inched closer like she hadn't noticed. Tae reviewed in her own thoughts how he hadn't broached the subject of her being his wife again, but they were in the act of moving in together. Jax seemed to think that settled things. She saw it differently.

Tae waited until he drew up in front of her and rested his hands on her waist, and his gaze locked onto her heavy breasts. "Jax?"

"Hm?" His response was more a moan than anything else.

"Do you love me?"

He stilled and looked up at her. "How could you ask me that?"

"It's a question, Jax. Do you love me? If I weren't pregnant, would you be with me?"

"Tae…"

"I don't like that I have to ask you."

He released her waist and backed up. Her heart faltered. "I'm not like Daniel, Tae."

Let me die right now. I can't deal with this. No, that's selfish. She shut her eyes and turned away. Her robe lay across the bed. She walked over to it and drew it on. Jax moved up behind her and helped her get her arms into the robe. He turned her shoulders and closed the garment, then belted it around her wide middle.

She didn't know she had started to cry until he brushed a thumb across her cheek to wipe away a tear.

"We were great friends," he said. "You and I would laugh and act stupid while Daniel was the mature one. We made fun of people when we were all out at a restaurant or went bowling."

"That's when you didn't have your tongue down some woman's throat. I realize I'm probably cramping your style."

"You *are* my style. Now."

She cast him a confused glance. He led her to the rocking chair he'd bought a month ago and sat down in it then drew her onto his lap. Jax had told her he intended to sing to their baby in the chair. She had informed him he couldn't hold a tune. He insisted he would give it a go. She'd pray for their poor baby.

"We both had to change over the last few months because of our own choices," he explained. "You didn't intend to have kids, and I didn't either, but we both want Little Jaxon, right?"

She smiled. They had decided on that too, giving the baby Jax's name. He would be a junior. "Yes, we do."

"I don't regret those changes at all. I'm not missing my old job." He held her face between two big palms to keep her focused on him. "I'm not missing sleeping with a different woman every other day."

"You were that much of a whore?"

He grinned. "Focus, woman."

"Trying."

"If you didn't get pregnant, I'd still be wanting to get in your panties, but I'd never approach you because of Daniel. If I felt like I do now back then, I would drop him in a heartbeat to get you. I have always wanted you, but the feeling has only grown."

She gaped.

"What I'm saying is, I love you more than life. I can't promise to say it every day or even often, because I can feel my face on fire telling you now. But I do love you, Tae. You and Jaxon are my entire world, and I'll give up anything and anyone to keep you. Do you understand?"

She nodded slowly, shocked beyond belief. The intensity in him blew her away. He wasn't just spewing out words. His love seemed to go as deep as Daniel's had, maybe even deeper. Tae lay on his shoulder and wrapped her arms around his neck. "I love you too, Jax. I have for a long time. Over these past months, we've developed, and you're right, we changed, and we see the world differently. Little Jaxon did that for us, and I'm glad of where we are. Once upon a time, my career was the most important thing. Now I can't wait until we bring him home to the nursery we set up at your house."

"*Our* house." He fidgeted beneath her, and she wondered if she was getting too heavy. "Tae?"

"Do you want me to get off your lap?"

"No, I want you to look up."

She yawned and opened her eyes. When had she even shut them? Seeing what he held in his hand brought the squeal she'd expected months ago. "Is that…?"

Jax popped the tiny black box open to reveal a dazzling diamond ring. "Tae, will you marry me?"

"You're slow, Jaxon Hart!"

He winked. "I'm always on time."

"Yes," she breathed. "Yes, I will marry you. Yes, yes, yes!"

He slipped the ring on her finger and raised her hand toward his mouth. A flick of movement and he pressed his lips to her inner wrist. Her pulse raced out of control, her pussy clenching.

"My wife," he murmured.

Tae melted against his chest. "Were you always confident I

loved you or that I would choose you because you always seemed like it?"

"Of course."

She smacked his arm. "Liar."

"Okay, I thought about what I would do if you left me for Daniel."

Tae saw the pain in his expression and the way he gripped the chair's arm. She stroked his chest and kissed him. "It's okay because I chose you."

"Good girl."

She smirked.

"You love him though, don't you, Tae?"

"I did. I guess I kind of love him now, but I'm not in love with him anymore. He wasn't the right one. I made that decision years ago, and this situation showed me I was right. Daniel is a great man. He really is, but not *my* great man." She had never told Jax how Daniel basically threatened her and made her feel like she didn't have a choice about being with him. Jax would have confronted Daniel, and things were bad enough with him knowing Daniel lied about him giving up on her and the baby. How Daniel thought he would get away with such a lie, she had no idea, but it caused a greater rift between them and with her and Daniel. In a way, she felt sorry for him. He was alone, without her, Alise, and Jax. Someone was always going to come out of this situation hurt. That was the nature of their tug-of-war, but she hoped more than anything that Daniel would some day find happiness again and let her go.

Jax tapped her hip. "Hungry? I was thinking of trying out a new recipe."

"Aren't we supposed to be finishing up with the moving?"

"What's this we you speak of, woman? You haven't lifted a lamp."

She snorted. "Whose fault is that? If I break a nail, you throw a hissy fit."

He flared his nostrils. "I do not throw hissy fits."

Tae laughed at the offense in his bearing and climbed off his lap. Behind her, Jax grumbled.

"You will be punished severely one of these days."

She spun to face him and flashed her boobs. His eyes glittered. She started to hurry away when a stabbing side pain stopped her cold. The next instant they both stared at the wet spot on the carpet beneath her feet.

"Jax! My water—"

"—just broke!" he finished. "Your bag is ready by the door. I'll carry you to the car and come back up for it."

"I can walk."

He would hear no arguments, and they rushed out of the apartment. Before long, Tae lay in a hospital bed breathing through the pain. Zerita held her hand, encouraging her, and Jax stood on the other side, wiping her forehead. "Not long now, sweetie," Zerita said of the contractions being five minutes apart. "You're almost there."

Tae moaned. "Did anyone call my mother?"

"I did," Jax said. "She and your dad are going to fly down."

Hours later, after agony that felt like it would rip her sanity away, Tae gave birth to her sweet baby boy. She slept like the dead for a while and next opened her eyes to see her mom not far away, cooing to the baby in her arms. Tae turned her head, yawning to find Jax sitting on her other side, his hand in hers and him fast asleep.

"Looks like you found a good one," her mother said.

Tae smiled, not taking her eyes off Jax. "I did."

"What's my grandson's name?"

"Jaxon Devlin Hart, Jr."

Zerita pushed open the door. "Wow, Devlin? For real?"

Tae laughed. "Yes, don't make fun of my husband's name or my son's."

"Ohh, somebody acts like nobody ever had a man or a baby but her."

Tae snorted. "Don't hate."

"Ladies," her mother interrupted. "Do not use that disgusting slang around this infant. He will grow up to be a very intelligent gentleman, who is successful in his career and life."

Zerita met Tae's eyes, and they both smiled. Tae's mother always acted this way when a grandchild was born. She'd never thought her baby would be a part of the ritual. "You're right, Ma, but what I want most for Little Jaxon is that he is happy and that he is loved."

"He is loved, just like his mother."

At Jax's voice, Tae turned back to him. His eyes were red with rings around them from lack of sleep. He'd seemed to go through as much as she during her labor and delivery. Through it all, he stuck by her. *I can't believe how blessed I am.* "You should go home and rest," she suggested to him.

"I will in a little while."

Zerita kissed her cheek. "I'm going to go. If you need me, just call." She leaned closer and whispered in Tae's ear. "Your mom saw the rock."

Tae groaned. She turned to her fiancé. "Baby, I want you to go get something to eat in the cafeteria."

He was about to protest but seemed to pick up on what she wanted. He nodded, kissed her lips, kissed their son's cheek, and left. Tae's mother brought the baby to her as he started to fuss. "I think he's hungry, Tae. Are you breastfeeding?"

"Yes, Jax and I discussed it. We thought I'd give it a try. If Little Jaxon tries to kill me, I'm going to the bottle in a hot minute."

Her mother frowned at her attitude but nodded. They sat in silence while she fed the baby, and Tae glanced at the shimmering ring on her finger. Since she moved to Charlotte, she and her mom didn't have a great relationship. Talking to her on the phone about the pregnancy resolved that issue as much as it could be resolved. Her mother still felt betrayed, but at least she wasn't crying anymore.

"Ma, I was wondering if you would consider planning my wedding. I know you're good at that sort of thing, and it just wouldn't turn out as well if you're not the one handling it." She prayed this olive branch would not turn out to be a big mistake.

Her mother pressed both hands to her chest. "Do you mean it, Tae? I saw the ring, and I thought you left me out of your life again."

"No, I didn't. I just knew you would come down here, and I wanted to talk about this face-to-face." This was true, mostly. She had seen no other way to handle the situation. "I don't want anything huge, just something for the family and our closest friends. I never thought I'd get married, but now I think nothing would make me happier than being Mrs. Jaxon Hart. I want it to be special."

Tae held her breath, waiting for her mother's response. In truth, while she still valued her personal space when it came to her family, she did want her mother's involvement—*controlled* involvement. She wanted her son to know his grandparents and extended family.

When her baby was done eating, she eased him to her shoulder and patted his back. Bright eyes blinking as he yawned, Little Jaxon was the spitting image of his daddy. Tae ran her fingers through the silky, dark hair and noted the shape of the baby's nose and jaw, and the color of his eyes. All of it was Jax's. She'd only contributed the light caramel color of his skin.

Her mother clapped her hands, capturing Tae's attention just as the baby burped. "I know just what we'll do, Tae. Your wedding will be talked about for years to come. All of my friends will be jealous."

"Your friends?" Tae chuckled, but she let her mother talk. They were good for now.

❦

Tae left the doctor's office for her checkup feeling on top of the world, or as on top of it as she could get with a baby who still woke in the middle of the night, breaking her sleep. She didn't care about that though. Dr. Chen had given her the green light. She and Jax could get as physical as they wanted, and since her mother had come down to handle some more details of the wedding in person, she had agreed to watch the baby for Tae that night. Thank goodness her mother didn't ask for details of what Tae planned for her and Jax. He didn't know them either. In fact, she'd lied and told him her appointment was on Thursday. The man backed off enough for her to drive herself and Little Jaxon wherever they needed to go, but he still hovered. She wanted to surprise him.

And surprised my man will be when he gets a load of my new outfit. Let the punishment begin!

She buckled the baby into his seat with a grin on her face, kissed him because he was so darn cute, and shut the door. When she turned to go around to her side of the car, her steps faltered, and the smile faded. Her heart pounded, and her eyes widened. "Daniel."

"Hello, Tae. It's good to see you."

She looked past him, not knowing what or who she expected to see but saw no one. "What are you doing here?"

"I figured you kept the same doctor. You don't live in the apartment anymore. You weren't at your job."

She frowned. "You've been checking up on me?" If he'd gone to the magazine and asked around about her, he might have run into Zerita, but she'd talked to her friend last night, and Zerita said nothing about seeing Daniel.

He stuffed his hands into his pockets and rocked back on his heels. Tae thought he looked thinner, a lot thinner. His skin was a tad sallow, and dark rings circled his eyes. Daniel always kept his hair in perfect order, but today it appeared greasy and messy. Hard wrinkles marred the shirt he wore even if his slacks looked okay. Well, it was late afternoon, so maybe he'd had a difficult day at the office.

"I'm not allowed to come to your house."

"Did Jax say that?" Daniel would know where Jax lived. Jax had owned the house for ten years.

Daniel produced a sad smile that tugged at her heart. "He doesn't want you tempted."

"Jax trusts me. He knows I wouldn't cheat on him."

Now Daniel frowned. "Have dinner with me."

"You know I'm not going to do that."

He held up a hand. "Not…as an ex-lover but as a friend. I'm not trying to get back with you. I just…"

"What, Daniel? What are you trying to do? You and Jax aren't friends anymore, and that breaks my heart."

"I lov—" He cut himself off and sighed looking away. "I want my old friends back. I have no one anymore. You know how my parents are, and the divorce with Alise was finalized a couple weeks ago. For a little while we tried to make it work, but every time I looked at her, I saw you."

"Daniel, don't."

He fell silent. Her heart wrung for him. Not because she still loved him, but because he didn't deserve this. If she hadn't hooked up with his best friend, at least he'd have Jax by his side.

"Why don't you come to dinner tomorrow night? If you concentrate on rebuilding your friendship with Jax, everything will work out between you."

He looked so hopeful. Tae knew she'd made the right decision.

"Tomorrow at six thirty, okay?"

He nodded. "Thanks, Tae."

"And Daniel?"

"Yes?"

She pointed a finger at him. "Come correct. That's all I'm saying."

"I will. See you tomorrow."

Tae watched him walk away and wondered how she'd break the news of their guest to her fiancé. Well, maybe he'd be more inclined to forgive his friend after tonight's activities. She grinned in anticipation as she slid behind the wheel of her car and headed home.

Chapter Sixteen

Tae stepped out of the shower, wrapped a towel around her, and ran on tiptoe to her ringing cell phone. She'd just missed Jax's call. Before she could call him back, his text came in.

"Stopping at Walgreen's. Be there shortly. Need anything?"

She chewed her lip, thinking about it. If she said condoms, he'd know what she had planned, but she wasn't on the pill because it made her sick. She opened the top drawer of his dresser and rummaged around. As luck would have it, he had three in there.

"Just a bottle of sweet tea if you don't mind. You know the flavor I like."

"Breastfeeding mommy."

She grumbled. *"I can have one or two cups a day, Daddy!"*

"Lol."

She rolled her eyes at the phone and dropped it on the nightstand. After moisturizing her skin with a gold glitter lotion, she slipped into a purple lace chemise. The underwire black lamé cups would support her boobs while still looking supersexy, and the lamé lace-up front hid the problem area of her belly. She tried on sheer thigh-high stockings with garters, but the elastic pressed too much into her thick thighs and looked like they were choking off circulation. She discarded them and opted for just a strip of cloth that constituted panties. Six-inch clear platform sandals completed her outfit. Jax's horny ass would love it, she was sure.

As she waited for her fiancé, Tae wandered from the living room to the kitchen to the bedroom. Jax's house as he said was small, but it was cute with three bedrooms and in a quiet Concord neighborhood. All she'd needed to know was that it was a short drive to Concord Mills Mall. She loved it on sight and felt that it would do very well for their little family.

When she picked up the sound of Jax's car in the driveway, she ran to the couch and sat down, then jumped to her feet and almost fell on her face in the high heels. She pressed a hand to her chest. "Calm down, idiot. You are not brand new."

She took a deep breath and then struck a pose beside the couch, feeling like an amazon in the heels. Jax stuck his key in the door, turned the lock, and strode in. The two bags in his hand slid to the floor with a *thunk*.

"I hope you didn't break my bottle of tea," she said.

He stared at her, his mouth agape, eyes like they'd pop out of his head. Then he realized he held the door open, scooped up the bags and hurried in to slam the door. "Tae, what are you wearing?"

She widened her eyes. "What do you mean?"

"Where's Jaxon?"

"My mom's keeping him for the night."

A slow grin spread over his face. "Is that so?"

"Yes."

"And the outfit?" His hot gaze seemed to sizzle as it traveled down her legs to her feet. The polished toes did look cute. "Those shoes?"

"I'll take them off if you want. They do make me really tall." She started to bend down.

"If you do, I'll spank you." He crooked a finger at her. "What am I saying? I owe you a spanking anyway."

"I don't know what you're talking about, sir."

"Wetting my clothes. I have a good memory, Tae, and I meant to take you over my knee."

She folded her arms across her chest. "Whatever."

"Get over here." He pointed to the spot on the floor in front of him. "Right here."

"What will happen if I don't?"

"By all means, please disobey me."

She bit her bottom lip. All kinds of fantasies played out in her head. How far would Jax take it? She knew he liked it rough. That first time having sex with him had been so different from what she was used to, and he'd been pinning back most of his preferences while she carried their son. Now she was good to go, he could unleash. The knowledge both thrilled and terrified her.

Just to see what he'd do, she sashayed across the room and stood where he indicated. Her heart did a flip-flop as she looked up at him. Yeah, up. Jax was still taller. Damn, she loved her man.

"Here, Daddy?" she said, her voice low and sultry. She reached out to touch a finger to his chest and played with the top button on his shirt. A tilt of her head and a single bat of her lashes had a muscle in his jaw twitching. She didn't need to look down below to see if he'd grown a hard-on. While she hated parts of her body, she didn't doubt Jax wanted her. Tonight he would eat her up, and she couldn't wait.

For a moment Jax seemed to fight his response, and then he went calm, no expression on his face. He pushed a hand in his pocket and stepped back from her. "Pick up those bags and take them in the kitchen."

She bent to do his bidding.

"No, not like that." He twirled his finger pointing downward. "Turn around and spread your legs. Don't stoop."

Picking up his meaning didn't take much imagination, and she was glad she'd worn the panties. Then again, nothing at all would have worked too. She moved around in front of him and spread her legs. Bending at the waist, she gathered the bags but took her time about it. Jax's gaze locked on her ass. He studied her like a science experiment, pressing fingers to his mouth, expression serious.

"Mm, that's right," he commented. A smack on her cheeks made her start. "Get in there."

She handled the chore and set the bags down. A quick peek in the bag showed he hadn't bought the tea. Bastard would pay later. He was still overly protective, and now it extended to Little Jaxon.

"Tae."

Jax called her from the bedroom. She joined him there. He had brought a scuffed treasure chest out from somewhere. The thing looked like an antique with its scratches, dents, and tarnished gold lock. "We need to have a little discussion, my love."

Tae licked her lips and swallowed. She took her time approaching him. "We do?"

The whip in his hand, no more than a foot in length from handle to tassels, was smooth and soft when she touched it, but there wasn't a doubt in her mind that it could cause a good sting. Jax lowered his hand and touched the whip between her legs. He ran it along the silk panties at her crotch, and she moaned, catching his arm.

"I said I'm going to spank you. I can use this or my hand, or any number of other toys I have in here."

She peered into the chest and caught her breath. "Um, did you use this on other women?"

"This entire chest is compiled for you, Tae. All of the toys are new, and I've been collecting them while I waited."

Her heart threatened to jump from her chest. The little panties were pretty much gone. "The box looks old."

"I inherited it from Dad."

"If he only knew how depraved his son was, he would have rethought that gift."

Her sass got her a swat on the ass with the whip. She yelped at the sting. Jax used the whip to raise her chemise. "Take off the panties."

"I thought we were going to talk."

Another swat. She was good and truly wet, and bent to take off her panties. Jax moved behind her so he could watch, and she was sure to give him a show. The whip grazed her wet lips, and she moaned.

"What else do you have?" she asked when she was done taking off her panties."

He cupped her chin and kissed her. "You really want to know? Does me taking control of you turn you on, baby?"

"You know it does."

"And if I were to cuff you to that hook and not let you down while I eat your pussy?"

She examined the wall where he indicated and wondered when he'd placed the hook there. "What part of that needs to be discussed?"

He whipped her. She whimpered. He pulled her to his chest. "It's not all fun and games for you, little one. You have to please me."

"What do I have to do?"

"You need to undress me precisely the way I tell you to. Understand?"

"Yes."

The whip stung her cheeks. "Yes, sir. Yes, Jax. Or yes, Daddy."

She gasped and smiled. "Yes, Daddy."

His cock twitched behind his pants. "Good girl. Do you want to play? Is this toy fine with you?" She confirmed in the way he had instructed her, and he held up cuffs. She licked her lips and confirmed again. The last item he displayed she had no clue about. When she frowned in confusion, he explained. "You're grabby. This little device will constrain you in an interesting way. It's called thigh cuffs. It will lock your hands to your thighs. This other one will latch your wrists to your ankles. I may or may not alternate between the two tonight. You've shown me that pretty pussy. I think I will have to use one or both."

Tae warmed from the top of her head to her feet. "I want it. I want everything you have for me."

He squeezed one of her breasts gently and then dragged down the material of her chemise to expose the nipple. A bit of milk leaked from the tip, and she grumbled. Jax tsked and caught the drop on his tongue. His moan sent shivers up and down her back. He sucked her tiny peak, easing the ache in it, but before she could sink into the pleasure he gave her, he stepped away.

"Don't stop," she complained. *Thwack!* She cried out. "I'm sorry, Jax."

"You will learn, won't you?"

"Yes, sir."

He shifted the chest to the floor and set the whip on the bed with the other toys he'd removed from it. Then he stood in front of her. "Unbutton my shirt now."

She moved to obey. Following each instruction the way he gave it, she managed to get him down to his boxers. Jax put his hand in the way so she couldn't lower them. "No, I want you to pull my cock through the opening."

She went to do it, but he stopped her again.

"On your knees."

Tae dropped down and raised her hands. She blinked when he clamped cuffs on her wrists. With limited movement, she would have to give extra effort to please him. An aching need to do just that came over her, and she glanced up at him. Jax had maintained a firm command over himself and his reactions up until that moment, but for a second as she studied his face, his mask melted away, and she saw his love. *Her Jax*, who found it hard to admit his feelings, adored her. Her heart swelled, but something told her now wasn't the time to go all mushy on him. He needed her to be obedient.

"How do you want me to do it, Daddy?"

He smiled and stroked her cheek. "Good girl. Reach in with both hands and bring it out."

She did.

"Do you want to suck it?"

Yes, she told him. In fact her mouth watered. Jax's cock had gone so solid, so much bigger than it usually was. She had a feeling seeing her cuffed and at his mercy got him that way. The tip of his cock spilled a bit of precome.

"Lick it."

She did and took the head between her lips. Her presumptuousness got her punished, and she whimpered. Jax made up for his cruelty teasing her nipples. Her pussy pulsed, wanting him to satisfy her already, but he held off. She had to do what he wanted step by torturous step.

He grabbed her chin and raised it. "Look at me, Tae."

She lifted her gaze to meet his. "We both like it rough. Me probably a little more than you, but I always want you to feel safe. You understand?"

When she told him she did, he continued.

"We need a safe word for if you get to where it hurts too much or we're doing something you're not comfortable with. As soon as you say the word, baby, I stop. Period. No questions, no pressuring you to continue. Even if my balls are exploding."

She grinned. He ran the pad of his thumb over her lips, and she kissed it, Then realized she probably shouldn't have done that without his permission. He winked. "We're pausing for a minute."

She blew out a breath of relief, although a little disappointed that she hadn't been spanked. The glimmer in his eyes said he knew she liked it and he'd give it to her soon.

"Think of a word that's easy for both of us to remember," he instructed. "It cannot be *stop* or *no.*"

Tae frowned in concentration. Then the perfect word came to her. "How about potato?"

Jax's brows shot up, and she thought he'd laugh but he nodded. "Potato it is." His playful expression disappeared. "Suck my cock, Tae. Do it now."

He still held her chin, leading her to his hard-on. She opened her mouth, and Jax pushed forward. The bulbous head slid into her mouth, and she tasted precome, salty and good. She sucked hard, producing a moan from her lover. He pressed until his cock touched the back of her throat, then withdrew. Slowly, he backed her up until her head rested on the end of the bed. She raised her hands to hold his cock, but he clicked with his tongue.

"Down."

She put her hands in her lap, and Jax bent his knees. He began a slow pump into her mouth, one that picked up speed. The head of his cock touched the back of her throat, but didn't hurt her. She kept her lips wrapped around him as he did all the moving. His ball sac bumped her chin, and he fell forward, bracing himself on the bed. His hips arched, driving him back and forth. When he groaned, his movements stilled, and he pulled out, panting.

"That hot mouth is going to make me come."

"I thought that's what you wanted."

He tapped her lips with a finger. She knew to shut up. "Not yet. If we don't stop, I will be finish before I get in you, and that's not going to happen. Stand up."

She rolled over, and he helped her to her feet. He unlocked the cuffs and tossed them aside, but he had a new restraint waiting.

"Bend over and put your wrists next to your ankles on the inside. You can rest your head on the bed if you like."

Goose bumps broke out on Tae's arms and legs. Jax's hair brushed the back of her leg as he locked the cuffs onto her wrists and ankles. When he was done, she couldn't raise her hands or straighten. A sliver of fear raced down her spine. If she said potato, would he release her? Just as she considered this, Jax's hands came up to her waist, and he leaned around so she could see his face. He stilled, looking into her eyes. The gentlest of expressions came over his features. This was her man, and he had never done anything she didn't like. If he did, he was quick to make it right. She trusted him, or she never would have allowed him to cuff her.

"Good?" he whispered. The man read her like a book.

"Yes, Jax." Her voice came out breathy and sexy. Jax grinned. He kissed her lips and smacked her ass with the flat of his hand before stroking her stinging skin. His fingers crept between her crack and lower to skim her pussy. All he had to do was part her opening and he'd glide right in she was so wet, but he held her nether lips apart and gave her a long lick. Tae shuddered, moaning. She clamped her teeth together to keep from begging him for more. He pushed his tongue into her pussy and wiggled it around. The cry of pleasure escaped before she could catch it. Jax squeezed her cheeks and dragged her backward to his hungry mouth. When he moved to her clit and teased it with the tip of his tongue, her knees buckled. He drew away. *No!*

"Straighten up," he commanded.

Tae did as he asked and received the reward of being thoroughly eaten until her muscles quivered, and her breath hitched. She screamed his name, and when she begged him not to stop, he spanked her good. Jax lapped her dripping juices and moved to her cheeks. He nipped her skin, making her whimper. Running his hands up and down her thighs, he kissed her all over the backs of her legs, her hips her butt and worked his way up until he stood behind her.

Tae's legs shook, and Jax grasped her hips in a strong hold. He dragged her backward and impaled her on his hard shaft. He thrust, and his entry forced her walls to stretch, accommodating him. The ache made her hotter. She arched her back as well as she could from the awkward position, straining at the bonds. Jax swatted her ass and jerked her back again. He plunged his cock deeper. Her mouth fell open, and she sucked in great gulps of air.

"You made me wait a long time, Tae," he scolded.

"I'm sorry."

He pulled out and thrust in again, harder and faster. Her pussy pulsed and clenched internally to squeeze his cock. Jax howled his pleasure.

"You're going to pay for making me wait, baby."

"Yes," she pleaded.

Jax started out slow and then pounded into her pussy, grinding deep as he held her around the waist like a vise. The slap of their flesh coming together over and over hypnotized her. The sensations mounted until she couldn't think straight. Jax's angry grunts filled the room, but he kept strong control over himself and her body. She shouted through another release, and Jax pulled out of her. He fought with the lock on her ankles and wrists, desperate to get them off. When he did, he tossed her on the bed like she weighed nothing and followed her.

"Arms above your head!"

She raised them and clutched the sheets in her fingers. Jax leaned on one hand and put a knee on the bed. He guided his throbbing cock to her pussy and plunged inside. A curse dropped from his lips as he'd pounded into her sore snatch only three times before he came. He sagged down against her and kissed the back of her neck.

"You're so beautiful. I can't get enough of your body."

He rolled to the side, and she turned over to settle into his embrace. "Did I please you, Daddy?"

He groaned. "Oh so well, baby."

Tae raised her knee and ran her toes up and down his leg. She wrapped her arms around his neck and nibbled his bottom lip. Jax breathed hard. She felt moisture beneath her fingertips on his skin, and when she leaned back she enjoyed the sight of his chest rising and falling and his flat, hard belly sinking in and out.

She grazed the delicious flesh, loving the feel of her fiancé. He wasn't the only one who couldn't get enough. How did she end up with a man like him? Either way, she'd do all she could to keep him and spend her life showing him what he meant to her.

"Jax?"

"Hm?" He'd shut his eyes and yawned.

"I uh...I need to tell you something."

"What's that, baby?"

"Jax." She shook him as he drifted off. "Wake up. I have to tell you something."

He seemed to force his eyes open. "I'm awake. Is it my turn to get the baby?"

She laughed. "You know before I got pregnant we went all night long."

He grinned. "You mean in the hotel. Mm, yes. Remembering gets me hard."

He wasn't lying by the nudging at her belly.

"When Little Jaxon sleeps all night, we'll have to reenact that night."

She purred. Jax squeezed the back of her thigh and headed up toward her pussy, but she covered his hand. "Wait, I need to tell you."

He paused.

"I invited Daniel to dinner tomorrow night."

Jax shot to the side of the bed. "You did what?"

She sat up. "I didn't think it would do any harm. You two were friends for years before I came along. I want you to talk."

He stood and walked around the bed to the dresser. When he brought shorts from a drawer, he stuffed his feet into them and jerked them up his legs. Tae half worried about his anger and half enjoyed the view.

"What were you doing seeing him?"

She forgot about his legs. "I was not 'seeing' him as you put it. I ran into him while I was out. I invited him. He's coming, and if you want to continue to act like a butthead, you can while I enjoy my dinner and talk to your best friend."

Jax glared at her. "I thought this was a night for us to be together alone, and you bring him into our bed."

She stood and moved toward the bathroom. "Dramatic much?"

"Oh, damn!"

She turned around. "What?"

He held something he'd picked up from the dresser. "We didn't use a condom."

Chapter Seventeen

The *clink* of forks hitting plates, and throats swallowing wine were the only sounds in the dining room. Every now and then, Little Jaxon cooed as he kicked his tiny feet in his chair. Tae peeked beneath her lashes at Jax and then at Daniel. Neither man had spoken more than two words to the other.

"How do you like the steak?" she dared to ask Daniel.

He smiled and raised his fork. "Delicious. You're a good cook."

Jax flared his nostrils. "*I* cooked it."

Tae suppressed a chuckle, and Daniel reddened.

He set his fork down. "Then I guess it's not as good as I thought."

"Really?" Jax sneered.

"Don't start, you two," Tae warned. The tension mounted, and she wanted to scream that they both needed to stop acting like children.

The argument broke out full scale. Both men jumped to their feet, fists raised.

"You know you're pretty insecure for a man about to get married," Daniel taunted.

Jax bared his teeth. "You've never been able to get over that she preferred me."

Daniel looked at her and then back at Jax. "Her pussy—"

Jax's fist smashed into Daniel's face, and Daniel went down hard. His entire plate of food landed on his chest, and blood gushed from his nose. Jax leaped after him and grabbed his shirtfront, raising his fist a second time. Daniel seemed too stunned to react. Little Jaxon wailed, and Jax froze.

"You see what you did?" Tae rushed to take the baby from his seat, but Jax appeared at her side and brushed her hands away to do it himself. He had their son against his chest in a heartbeat, crooning to him and walking the floor. Daniel brushed food from his chest, wincing, and then stemmed the flow of blood as he rose from the floor. He flopped into his seat and watched as Jax walked back and forth. Tae grabbed a napkin and handed it to Daniel, and he looked at her.

"All this time, I assumed I would be better," he whispered.

Tae glanced at her fiancé, but Jax paid them no mind. She doubted he had heard Daniel. "Jax adores that little boy. He's a great daddy. We both love him so much."

Daniel said nothing. He stared down at the mess on the floor, his expression unreadable. When the baby calmed, Jax returned to the table, but he kept Little Jaxon in the crook of his arm. Tae resisted running to get her cell phone to take a picture. Jax claimed she had a thousand already. She'd called him dramatic again.

"Hey," Daniel said, capturing Jax's attention. He ran his hands through his hair, and Taw saw how Jax frowned at it. He too must have noticed the change in Daniel, and she sensed no malice in her fiancé. Daniel looked at his friend. "I want us to go back to being friends. I know she's yours now. I accept it. I'm not saying I don't feel anything, but I won't make waves."

Tae crushed her napkin beneath the table, staring at Jax. Talk about a quick about-face. Would Jax accept it?

Jax looked away from both of them. "Yeah, whatever. Sure, bro."

Tae beamed. "See? I knew you could patch things up. Now, give me the baby, Jax. You and Daniel can clean up my floor!"

Her fiancé frowned, but she whisked the baby away. The next item on her agenda was to get Jax to invite Daniel to the wedding.

❦

Tae stood at the back of the chapel, her stomach tied so tight in knots, she didn't know if she wanted to pass out or throw up. For some reason, all she could think about was the last wedding she attended and how everything went to pieces afterward. Daniel's marriage hadn't lasted five minutes, and there'd been so much between her, him, and Jax, how could she believe it would be okay this time around? Hadn't she started the relationship wrong with Jax? Shouldn't she still feel guilty?

The problem was, she didn't. The lack of guilt made her question herself now that she stood here. She shut her eyes and pressed a hand to her forehead, willing the emotions to die down. Her mother and Sasha had spent forever getting her face just right. No way would she cry before Jax saw her and mess it all up. On some level, she heard the violin, which they'd arranged to play during the ceremony, and recognized the "Wedding March." The beautiful melody flowed through her, reached the end, and started over again, and still she didn't move. A light hand at her back made her start.

"Tae, sweetie, we really should go in."

"I know, but what if he leaves me tomorrow?" The corners of her eyes moistened. She sucked in deep breaths. Her dad took both her hands and held them while he captured her gaze.

"Jaxon Hart loves you. That's why we're here. Besides that, you're a strong black woman. If he doesn't appreciate what he has in my little girl, he doesn't deserve you." Her dad released her hands and held up a finger. "And your mother will have his head for ruining what she calls her perfect work of art."

Tae laughed. "Of course. It's all Ma's planning. Thanks, Daddy. I feel much better."

He gave her a hug, and she kissed his cheek, and then she nodded to the attendant to open the chapel doors. Tae stepped into the long, narrow chapel with wooden, cushion-covered benches on both sides of the aisle. Her mother had arranged the decorations so that white streamers were pinned at each bench with a white bow. Sunlight shone through the stained glass windows, casting the scene of her husband to be, his best man, and the backdrop of the minister and bouquets of flowers into a warm and inviting cocoon.

Almost every seat in the chapel was filled, giving evidence to how her mother had ignored her wishes to have a small ceremony, but Tae looked beyond all the eyes observing her to meet the gaze of the one who mattered most. She knew Jax, and from the way he offered her that crooked smile with his shoulders too high and his hands fisted at his sides, she knew he was nervous, too. When she smiled back, something seemed to come over him. He relaxed, and unless she missed her guess, the man seemed love-struck.

As she moved along the aisle, she caught her mother's slightly raised voice telling the person next to her how she had picked out Tae's dress. That was true. Sasha and her mother both convinced her to buy the white dress with backline all the way down to her butt. Ruching extended over her butt to gather into a big white bow, sitting just beneath the curve of her rear. She loved the daring design, but it meant she'd had to exercise hard to get off the last few pounds, and she'd done it. If she did say so herself, she looked good, and Jax's response confirmed it.

Her mind a whirl, she went through the motions, lighting a candle, saying a prayer, but when he slipped the ring onto her finger and recited his vows, her attention was all on him.

"Octavia," he said softly. Jax never called her that. Her heart raced at the name from his lips. "When I met you, I fell in love."

Gasps broke out nearby, and a "knew that" from one of her family members. She couldn't take them anywhere.

"When I met you, you turned my life around. No other woman would ever satisfy me or make me happy."

She ducked her head at his candor, embarrassed and pleased. Jax sharing such deep feelings was a challenge, and she'd better remember the words forever. Wait, she had a man filming this. She'd have evidence.

"I knew you were the one, but…" For a millisecond, his gaze slipped to the side and then back on her. "The timing wasn't right." All of a sudden, Tae realized Jax was speaking of not when they had sex in the hotel but before that, long before that. He loved her from the first when she was with Daniel. Now he'd gone and done it. She started to cry.

The love of her life brushed her tears away, and the minister continued with the ceremony. Tae said her vows with all the honesty and love she had, gazing into Jax's eyes so he knew she meant it. Just as he had said to her, no other man could take his place or be the one like she knew he was. She hadn't loved Jax from the beginning, but that didn't matter. She would love him until the end of time.

The minister pronounced them man and wife, and Jax swept her off her feet into his arms. He kissed her so thoroughly, her veil slipped, and she smacked his shoulder. With cheers going up all around them, he set her on her feet, and they turned to face their guests. Tae caught Daniel's eye, and he offered a sad smile, applauding with everyone else. Between the two of them, he and Jax had agreed that they didn't feel comfortable for Daniel to act as Jax's best man, so Jax chose another friend, but Daniel had promised to be there. She was glad he'd kept his word.

Tae took in the sight of family and friends. With her husband by her side, she felt much more accepting of her mother's attitude and Janita's selfishness. Not that she intended to give in to it. She and Jax had enjoyed a few dinners with his dad, and she'd met his siblings. They were all nice and accepting of her. Tae had never thought being surrounded by family could mean so much, but she gave the credit to Little Jaxon and to his daddy.

"Ready?" Jax asked, bringing her hand to his lips.

She nodded. They worked their way through the guests, chatting, hugging, and kissing. When the crush was over, she and Jax took the baby to a room they had reserved at The Duke Mansion where they had arranged to have the reception. Tae laid the baby on the bed and kissed his sweet little cheek. Her baby cooed and kicked his feet. She breathed in the wonderful baby smell.

"Tae, let me help you with your dress."

She eyed Jax over her shoulder. "You know we have to go back downstairs for pictures, Jax. I'm not getting naked before that. I just came up here to freshen my makeup, and my mother is coming to get the baby."

He looked crestfallen. "But your back is driving me crazy."

She laughed. "It's called skin, sir."

He smacked her ass. "What about this?"

Tae darted away. "Stop, you're going to mess up my bow."

Jax snapped his fingers. "What do you say we go bowling later?"

"You're nuts."

"I can see you bowling in that dress. The shoes will match."

"Still crazy."

His hand came out of nowhere and landed on her waist to jerk her into his arms. "You love it."

Her breath caught in her throat as she looked up at him. Damn, getting manhandled could be hot. If she didn't get away from him, they really would be naked, and she could just see her mother knocking on the door while they scrambled to get something on. She wriggled in Jax's hold and bumped against his crotch. Resistance waned.

"You're hard," she accused.

He shrugged. "You're rubbing your pussy on it. How can I help it?"

"I am not rubbing anything on you, dirty-minded man."

"I wouldn't mind if you did."

"I bet. You've done enough damage. Now let me go."

Jax grinned, a self-satisfied look in his eyes. "Shall we tell them at the reception?"

She glared at him. "That we're going to have stepladder children? No! Well, maybe my mother and your dad to avoid the nonsense, but that's it. I hope I can handle this craziness."

He captured a tendril of hair that escaped her coiffure and brushed it to the side. "We will enjoy our children together. I'm your husband now, and you're my wife. I'll never leave you, Tae."

Her heart swelled, and she felt a tide of emotion she put down to being pregnant again so soon after having her first child. Jax knew her. The truth was, she didn't mind it at all. She adored Little Jaxon, more than she could have imagined, and she and Jax were pretty damn good at caring for him so far. They had learned a lot over the months of her pregnancy and worked to do better each day. She loved him, and he loved her. That's what was most important.

"I know," she said. "I'm happier than I've ever been, and I don't regret a thing."

He grinned. "Good. Now let me help you with your dress." His fingers slipped below the lining at her butt, and she smacked his hand. He frowned. "Tae."

A knock sounded at the door, and he fell silent. Tae slipped out of his hold. "Oh look at that. Too late. Come on, Jax. We have guests waiting for us."

He groaned. "Fine, but trust me, beautiful woman, you will make up for denying me."

She purred, thinking of the treasure chest. "Whatever you say, Daddy."

The End

About the Author

Tressie Lockwood is the best selling author of interracial contemporary and shifter erotic romance. She has always loved books, and she enjoys writing about heroines who are overcoming the trials of life. She writes straight from her heart, reaching out to those who find it hard to be completely themselves no matter what anyone else thinks. She hopes her readers enjoy her books. Visit Tressie on the web at www.tressielockwood.com or her blog at tressielockwood.blogspot.com.